The Mysterious Mesa

Ward Jackson was a man who could not turn his back upon the distant horizon, forever riding in search of what lay beyond. That is until the day when he rode out of lush forest to be confronted by a deadly desert plain. Out in the shimmering heat haze, Jackson saw something which drew him like a moth to a flame – a massive monolith waiting silently, luring him on and on. And, all the while, he remained unaware of the two killers tracking him and the remnants of the small army map-making patrol to the east.

Beneath that mighty rock lay a small oasis where, God willing, there would be water. But dangers lurked, for high on the mysterious mesa, Indians were watching and waiting.

A massacre seemed inevitable but who would survive?

The Mysterious Mesa

DALE MIKE ROGERS

A Black Horse Western

ROBERT HALE · LONDON

ISBN 0 7090 6845 X

Robert Hale Limited
Clerkenwell House
Clerkenwell Green
London EC1R 0HT

Typeset by
Derek Doyle & Associates, Liverpool.
Printed and bound in Great Britain by
Antony Rowe Limited, Wiltshire

Dedicated to Michael 'Apache' Patterson
and all my Tlingit Indian friends in
Juneau, Alaska

ONE

He wore a battered old hat which seemed to be part of his weathered spirit as it moulded itself to the shape of his once noble head. His clothes were comfortable but, like himself, now showed their age by their almost colourless appearance. The sun had bleached them whilst tanning his skin almost to the shade of saddle-leather.

This was no ordinary man who sat astride his ageing grey mount; this was a rider who had once been on a mission, but who now simply continued riding towards a distant horizon which never seemed to get any closer.

There had been so many dreams. So many unfulfilled hopes of attaining the impossible. So many things which now appeared to be, like the heat haze before him, just a mirage. The rider who had been driven to leave the safety and normality of a life which he knew led to only one certainty, his own peaceful death from boredom in old age, wondered what kept him forging on.

Yet he had always felt his own destiny calling to him on the subtle breezes which came from beyond his fellow man's limited imagination.

Fate knew his weaknesses and lured him on and on into the unknown. He had never questioned anything and always complied willingly. Only his awareness of the fact that he was no longer as young as he had once been, now began to trouble him. The hairs on the back of his tanned hands were now white, like most of the other hairs on his body.

His youth might have deserted him but not his blind faith in what waited for him out there.

Now every sinew in his tired body told him there was little time left. A dozen years had seen the rider cross many borders but none to compare with the one which he now faced. If this place had a name, it was unknown to the man who sipped at one of his full canteens as his eyes traced the unfamiliar landscape.

It had to be out there, he thought.

Out there beyond the heat haze.

So many miles seeking something which he now began to realize could not be found as easily as he had once imagined. So many long hard trails had delivered him to this place and he knew this was probably his final chance of finding answers to so many confused questions.

Ward Jackson looked out across the vast sunbaked desert before him and tried to focus his tired eyes. Whatever it was out there beyond the endless miles of shimmering white sand, he could only guess at.

How far was it to the other side? There was no certain way of judging the distance but this did not trouble the rider. All he knew for certain was there was no turning back. Whatever it was he had so desperately sought, was not behind him. It still might be ahead of him though.

Out there.

It was as if he could hear it calling to him.

Only travelling forward could bring the answer he yearned for. Jackson knew it was far too late to turn back now even though he was faced with unknown dangers.

A baking hot desert of endless sand and no shade would have discouraged any rational rider but not Jackson. Life was nothing more to him than a roll of the dice, a calculated risk worth taking. Death held no fear for him because he had never acknowledged it.

Pulling his cracked leather gloves over his

hands, Jackson gritted his teeth and squared up to the strange sight of a shimmering merciless land. He looked around at the miles of tall trees through which he had journeyed for over ten days and at the pure clean water which flowed in the narrow winding river behind him. He patted the four full canteens which hung at either side of his saddle horn. He was ready.

He had never shunned danger in all the days of his fruitless quest, but the white featureless plain which he faced made him uneasy. Would four canteens be enough? He thought. They always had been, but he had never faced anything so unpredictable before. So silently awesome in its magnitude.

Whatever it was that danced in the moving heat which taunted his bloodshot eyes, still tormented Jackson. It was like watching a ghost mocking him from beyond the grave yet the weary rider seemed unable to take his eyes from the mirage.

If the answers lay anywhere, it was there.

Tapping his spurs into the sides of his faithful mount, Ward Jackson left the safety of the lush shaded timberlands and began heading down into the arid plains. The horse walked carefully over the uneven ground as Jackson leaned back in his saddle. The heat grew in intensity with every stride the mature animal took. For the first time in over a month the rider undid his jacket studs and removed the heavy garment. Sweat began to trickle down his face from his hat band and drip on to his shirt.

He could feel the heat bouncing up off the ground as well as beating down on to his body. He had never experienced such a heat, it felt as if his clothes were burning against his flesh. The light dazzled his tired eyes and made his mount nervous as he continued to encourage it onwards.

Jackson untied his bandanna and wrapped it around his head above his eyebrows in an attempt to soak up the sweat which flowed from under his old hat.

'Keep going, boy,' he urged the animal beneath him, yet all he could do was sit and allow the horse to find its own pace. The shimmering image grew no clearer to his screwed-up eyes as they vainly squinted against the blinding sunlight which danced ahead of them.

With every beat of his heart, Jackson grew more and more convinced he was on the right trail at long last. He was finally on the verge of claiming his destiny.

Staring around, Jackson felt uneasy as he began to fully realize that nothing but sand filled this vast place. No blades of grass, no tumble-weed or sage lived here.

Only sand. White hot sand.

TWO

'Where in tarnation is the varmint going, Duke?'
professional gambler Billy Charles asked his
rugged cohort, Duke Walker, as he leaned on his
saddle horn and sucked reluctant smoke through
his badly rolled cigarette. Charles was a man
who prided himself on his skills with cards as
well as his array of weaponry but both had met
their match when they had encountered the
unassuming figure of Ward Jackson three weeks
earlier. Charles and Walker had roamed through
the West together for nearly eight years, plying
their trade and using every trick in their seemingly limitless arsenal. They had never entered a
saloon together. Never shown any hint of recog-
nition across the hundreds of card tables they
had visited over the years.

13

Eight years had honed the secret signals to such a precision that it was impossible for the unenlightened to spot anything the pair said to one another through their masterful facial and physical body movements. To the onlookers these were two total strangers who never appeared to acknowledge one another. It had always worked until they had encountered the quiet Ward Jackson. Somehow he had managed to beat them at their own game. If he had cheated, neither Charles's or Walker's trained eyes had spotted anything. Yet he had won and strolled away with their money. Charles had immediately made his indignation known to the quiet Jackson but the swiftness with which the older man had drawn his gun stunned and frightened the gambler. He had never seen anyone draw so keenly or effortlessly before. Ward Jackson was not a man to tangle with fairly.

To take his kind, you had to cheat.

Duke Walker dismounted and tossed his reins around a sapling before striding to the edge of the clearing set amid the tall straight trees. Rubbing the back of his right thumb over his month-old beard, he sighed heavily.

'He must have gone loco.'

'Nah, Jackson ain't loco, Duke,' Billy Charles said, shaking his head as he eased himself off his mount and gently lowered himself to the ground.

'No sane critter would ride out into that, Billy boy,' the older man grunted as he watched the rider heading further and further into the perilous plain. 'Look at it. Nothing but desert that goes on and on for ever.'

'I wonder where he's heading, Duke?' Billy Charles wondered aloud.

'That trail leads to only one place,' Walker responded.

'Where?'

'Hell.'

Billy had to shrug as he allowed the smoke to drift through his teeth. 'Make a camp-fire and fix us some vittles while I try and figure out a few things, Duke.'

Duke Walker gave a nod and began gathering kindling as he watched his partner staring out from their hiding place across the endless white sand.

'We gonna wait for him to come back, Billy?'

'He ain't ever coming back this way, Duke.' Billy Charles spat at the ground as he bit his lower lip. He knew in his bones the quiet Jackson was the sort of man who just kept moving in one direction.

Straight ahead.

Walker straightened up and looked hard at his

sharp-minded junior. His face held a question in every wrinkle not covered by facial hair.

'Ain't coming back? You sure about that, Billy boy?'

'One way or another, he ain't gonna return here.' Charles inhaled the smoke and tossed the cigarette butt on to the ground before pressing his boot on to it angrily.

Duke Walker dropped the pile of kindling on to the ground as he moved back to the side of his young companion. He raised a finger and lowered the tone of his voice.

'If he ain't coming back this way, how come we didn't kill him when we had the chance, boy?'

Billy sighed heavily. 'I figure the sun out there will do for him for sure, Duke. It ain't meant for no man to ride out into that kinda inferno and live to tell the tale.'

'But if Jackson don't come back, how are we gonna get our goods back, Billy?' Walker leaned down to look into the shrewd eyes of his companion.

'We'll just keep following him, Duke,' Charles retorted bluntly.

'What? Have you gone loco too?' Walker gasped as he digested his partner's words.

'Fix the fire like I told you.' Billy Charles pointed at the stack of kindling. 'I wanna eat some hot vittles before we head out after our friend.'

'Answer me, boy. Has you gone crazy like Jackson?' Walker grunted angrily as he pushed his face within inches of his partner's.

'I ain't crazy. I figure we'll head out after sunset and trail him across that stretch of sand. If we are lucky, he'll be deader than a turkey on Thanksgiving.' Charles held out a box of matches and smiled as the older man accepted them.

'How come he'll be dead?' Walker asked as he pulled a long match from the box.

'He's old. That sun will fry him up in a matter of hours.'

'Maybe.' Walker was not so sure.

'No man could live out there for very long, Duke.' Billy Charles began to grin as he visualized Ward Jackson lying out on the hot sand being torn to shreds by buzzards. 'There ain't a scrap of shade out there. Nothing to stop the sun from boiling Jackson's brain until it ain't no bigger than a pea.'

'Maybe so, but why didn't we just kill him earlier when we caught up with him?' Walker knelt down and started arranging the kindling into shape.

'Jackson ain't the sort of man you wanna fight fair, Duke.'

'Just 'cos he out-drawed ya?' Walker looked up into his companion's face. 'You could have taken him if—'

'Jackson was fast, Duke. You seen it. There ain't no way I'm gonna tangle with him face on.' Charles shook his head as he spoke.

Walker sighed. 'I figure we could have taken him days ago with a rifle shot.'

'So far he ain't got a clue we're on his trail,' Charles said coldly. 'To risk a long-distance carbine shot in the country we've been tracking him through wouldn't have been very smart, Duke.'

'How come?'

'We would have missed, that's why.' Charles pulled out his tobacco pouch from his vest pocket and withdrew a thin gummed paper as he began to try once again to make a reasonably shaped smoke. 'As long as Jackson don't know we are hunting him, we have the advantage. Without it, he could just wait for us and pick us off at will.'

'I guess so,' Walker reluctantly agreed.

'He's old but good with that gun of his.' Billy Charles knew what he was talking about. If there was one thing Charles did not wish to do, it was tangle with the strange loner.

'But he got our gear, Billy. Our money.' Duke Walker struck a match and watched as it immediately went out before pulling another from the box.

'He might argue that he won it fair and square, Duke.' Charles carefully poured the fine tobacco on to the cigarette paper.

'He might?'

'Damn right he would,' Charles snapped as he began trying to roll the paper with his fingers and thumbs without the tobacco falling out.

'But he cheated, Billy boy,' Walker griped as he struck another match and put its flame to the kindling.

'We were the ones who was cheating, Duke. Jackson just figured it out and turned the tables on us.' Billy Charles ran his tongue along the gum of the paper before completely rolling the cigarette.

'Ain't ever cottoned to cheats, Billy.'

'Not ones who are a tad better at it than us, anyways,' Billy grinned broadly.

'We really gonna go out there in that desert?' Walker asked nervously as he added more dry twigs to the fire.

'Yep. But we are going when there ain't no sun up in the sky, Duke.' Charles picked up one of the burning twigs from the fire and touched the end of his crude smoke. 'We will not get our bones fried like him.'

The Mysterious Mesa

'We sure is smarter than that old varmint, ain't we?' Walker chuckled as he fanned the flames of their camp-fire with his hat.

Billy Charles exhaled a long line of cigarette smoke from his smiling mouth as he kicked some logs and twigs towards his partner, before kneeling beside the older man.

'We are smarter than Jackson, ain't we, Billy?' Walker repeated his question as he expertly placed the wood on to the growing flames.

'I figure we are twice as smart as Jackson, Duke,' Charles said. His eyes looked into the fire and watched as it danced through the kindling.

'How come, Billy?' Duke Walker seemed encouraged by the words from his pal.

'There's two of us, ain't there?'

'Yeah.'

If Ward Jackson didn't have all their money in his saddle-bags, Billy Charles knew that he would not have tried to get within a hundred miles of the quiet rider.

THREE

It had been four desperately hot hours and Ward Jackson seemed no closer to the distant image bathed in swirling vapours of boiling air which taunted his sore eyes. He had never imagined such a devilish heat existed anywhere outside the depths of Satan's lair, yet it did. This place could have been hell itself as it sucked every ounce of moisture from the rider and his horse. The smell of his mount's hair singeing beneath the leather saddle began to fill Jackson's nostrils. They were being burned alive.

He stepped off the exhausted, lathered-up mount and he ran a hand down the wretched creature's neck before flicking the lather on to the flat white sand. Jackson took one of his canteens from the saddle horn and sipped the now warm liquid before removing his hat and dropping it in front of the horse's forelegs.

'Thirsty, old-timer? I sure am,' Jackson muttered.

He knelt down on the hot sand and carefully poured out half the contents of the canteen into his upturned hat. He waited as the thirsty animal drank. Staring back to where they had come from, Jackson found it difficult to see anything clearly any longer. Now the thousands of trees behind him appeared to have totally vanished in the strange hot air. There was a silence out here in the desert such as the rider had never experienced before. There needed to be life to make a noise, this place was devoid of anything living.

Jackson plucked his hat up off the sand when the horse had finished and placed it back upon his head before taking another small sip from the canteen. Then, looking down at the hot burning sand at his feet, he instinctively poured the remainder of the canteen's contents over each of his mount's legs in turn before vigorously rubbing them down.

He hung the empty canteen beside the trio of full ones and looked at the tired horse carefully. He took the reins in his hands and began to lead the animal onwards. Although he felt as if his lungs were filled with molten lava, Jackson knew the old horse would not last if it were forced to carry his weight as well as that of his saddle and tack.

The rider's high-heeled boots seemed to sink into the soft sand as he moved forward slowly with his horse in tow. Every step made both of them gasp as they continued heading towards their distant goal.

'Come on, boy. We gotta keep going,' Jackson said as he felt his lips drying with each passing second. He had heard tales of places such as this but never imagined any of those tall stories had any bearing on reality. Now he knew such yarns were not only true but deadly accurate. Mile after mile he staggered onwards, unsure as to whether he was heading in the right direction. Only when he stared over his shoulder and saw the tracks he and his ageing horse had left, did he manage to work out their course.

A less determined or spirited man might have been discouraged, but not Jackson. Every passing moment made him realize this was exactly the sort of place where a man such as himself might discover something no other rational person had even dreamt of.

A man content with his lot would never have ventured out into such a place as this. Whatever lay out there waiting to be discovered would not be found by cautious souls. It took his sort to face the unknown.

Here death hovered in the vapours of heat haze which scorched his lungs with every breath he took. He knew it was fatal for the unprepared to venture into such a place, but he was prepared.

Every sinew of his aching body told him he was close to his goal. Every heartbeat brought him closer. A dozen years of searching for his destiny was within his grasp as long as he kept his nerve and retained his belief.

Jackson could taste the heat burning his dry mouth as he walked on dragging the quiet horse behind him. He had three full canteens tied to his saddle but here water was the most precious of God's bounties. His horse would require the biggest share if it were to survive to carry him out of this place. Jackson vowed the faithful grey would not die of thirst, even if it meant him going without.

Mile after mile he kept walking. Deeper and deeper into a place where even birds did not venture. The sand before him was untouched by tracks of any description. He knew it was unlikely that any other man had ever come this way.

Perhaps he was the first man to have come this way since God or the Devil had created this place, he mused.

As he reached up and pulled the second canteen off the saddle horn, his attention was caught by something. Screwing up his burnt eyes, he tried to focus through the dishonest mirage. He unscrewed the stopper on the canteen, wet the palm of his dry hand and rubbed the refreshing liquid over his face.

'Am I seeing things?' the old man mumbled to himself as he repeated his actions and washed the tiredness from his eyes.

Raising a hand to shield his eyes from the blinding light, Ward Jackson paused and gazed into the fog of eddying haze and swallowed hard. It was like looking into a wall of moving water but for the first time he began to see a looming edifice beyond the terrifying mirage.

'See it, boy?' Jackson said to the horse. 'See it?'

FOUR

Night arrived very quickly. There seemed to be little or no dusk. No sooner had the sun set than a blackness enveloped the entire landscape. It was a large moon, not quite full, that cast its eerie light over the forest above the desert. There had been few words spoken whilst the pair of very different men ate their cans of hot beans and sipped at their coffee sweetened with canned milk. Walker licked the blade of his knife and returned it to its leather sheath hanging on his belt. Charles had preferred to pour his beans straight from the can into his mouth.

They tossed their empty bean cans to one side; then Billy Charles and his partner Duke Walker shook their tin cups and rose reluctantly to their feet. Charles poured what was left in the large

26

black coffee-pot over the flames as Walker began kicking dust over the small camp-fire.

Nothing was said as the pair patted their blankets on to the backs of their refreshed mounts. Only when their saddles had been secured and the cinch straps tightened did either man cast a look in the direction of the other. Billy Charles still seemed happy with his plan whilst the older, more cautious, Walker muttered continuously under his breath.

'You ready, Duke?' Charles pulled the drawstring of his tobacco pouch with his teeth and slid it into his vest pocket as his tongue traced along the gummed paper of his cigarette.

'Nope,' came the honest response.

Billy Charles edged his way around his horse until he was standing next to the troubled Walker and struck a match across his saddle. Raising the flame to the tip of his twisted cigarette he sucked in the smoke slowly.

'It'll work, Duke. There ain't no danger.'

'For all we know that damn desert is nothing but quicksand, Billy boy,' Walker snarled as he gathered up his long loose reins from the ground. His face was like stone in the light of the moon which managed to penetrate the canopy of branches above their heads.

Billy Charles had not given any thought to the

possibility of there being quicksand out there. He rubbed his chin as he considered the idea carefully.

'We might end up just sinking, boy.' Walker added fuel to his suggestion as he watched the face of his companion bathed in moonlight. 'You never thought about that, did ya? For all we know, Jackson might have sunk like a stone hours back.'

'Jackson wouldn't have ridden out there if he had thought there might be quicksand waiting for him,' Charles said coldly as he tried to reassure both Walker and himself with a grit in his tone that he did not usually favour.

'How would he have known?' Walker bellowed as he watched the smoke drifting from the mouth of his friend.

'Jackson's smart, Duke.' Charles bit on his lower lip. However much he hated the quiet man who had taken their grubstake in that fateful poker game, he could not help but admire his guts.

'You're smart but you never gave it no mind, did ya?'

'True. I never gave it no mind at all, Duke.' Billy Charles drew in on his smoke and stared at its glowing tip in his long fingers.

Walker swallowed deeply.

'I ain't afraid to admit it, I'm scared.'

'Of Jackson?' Charles asked.

'Him and that sand, Billy.' Walker rubbed the sweat from his brow with the back of his sleeve as he visibly trembled. 'I ain't never seen anything like that sand.'

'Me neither, Duke,' Charles admitted as he rested a hand on his partner's shoulder. 'But it's dark now. That desert is only dangerous to the likes of living critters when the sun is up in the sky blazing down. It can't hurt nobody after sundown.'

'Maybe so.' Walker sighed uneasily.

'Look, I'm scared too. But all we gotta do is follow the tracks he's left out there, Duke.' Charles picked a tobacco leaf off his tongue.

'You're a tad scared too, Billy?' Walker seemed surprised by his partner's blunt admission.

'Yep. But he's got our bankroll in his saddle-bags and we ain't rich enough to lose that kinda dough.' Charles moved alongside his mount with his reins in his hands. 'So I figure unless we bite the bullet and head on after him, we are gonna have to turn our hand at cattle-rustling to make some money.'

'This ain't cattle country,' Walker shrugged.

'Exactly. So we gotta follow Jackson.' Charles dropped the cigarette butt on to the ground and crushed it with his pointed toecap.

'Do you figure we can catch up with him and make it back here before sun-up?'

Billy Charles held on to his saddle horn, stepped into his stirrup and hauled himself up on to his horse. He stared out through the hundreds of trees between them and the desert without a hint of emotion upon his face.

'Answer me, Billy. Can we make it to him and back before the sun rises?' Duke Walker was no coward but he knew when a hand of cards ought to be folded. This was such a hand of cards.

'If the sand is firm, we can make good time.' Charles grinned as he stared out at the perilous view between the trees.

'I still don't figure he'll be dead,' Walker grunted. He took a bite of his chewing tobacco before hiding it back inside one of his numerous pockets.

'But he just might be asleep.'

Walker nodded. 'You're right. He could be asleep.'

'How long we known each other, Duke?' Billy Charles asked as he settled himself atop his mount.

'Years and years. Why?' Walker always got edgy when the younger man began asking questions such as this. He had a way of twisting things around to get his own way.

'I ever led you into a bad game?' Charles raised his eyebrows as he watched the worried face of his comrade.

'Once or twice.'

'Have I ever failed to get us out of trouble?'

Walker began to shake his head. 'You always managed to keep us in one piece, I guess.'

Charles smiled. 'Get mounted and we'll see if we can pick Jackson's bones before sunrise, Duke.'

Walker reluctantly stepped into his stirrup and hauled his heavy body on to his horse.

'I'm still not happy, Billy boy,' the bigger man admitted as he pulled his hat down over his furrowed brow. 'I got me a bad feeling about heading on out across that damn sand.'

'You and me both, Duke. The main thing is we are gamblers who are forced to play the hand fate has dealt us. No point griping about it.'

Charles kicked his spurs into his horse's flesh and rode through the tall trees before reaching the steep slope which led down on to the sand. Following a mere few yards behind, Walker steered his horse along until he drew level.

Both riders stared out at the vast panorama before them. The moon made it all appear blue and cold. A million tons of sand stretched as far as their eyes could focus, like a peaceful ocean.

Only the tracks left by Ward Jackson marred its perfection as they headed out into infinity.

'Can you see him, Billy?' Duke Walker asked vainly as he rubbed his tired eyes with his bandanna. 'My old eyes ain't good at distance.'

'Nope. All I see is one heck of a lotta sand,' Charles said as he gave his horse another reminder to continue walking out into the soft desert.

'How long do you reckon we got?'

'I figure there's about eight hours before sun-up,' Billy Charles said quietly as he held his reins up to his chest and allowed his horse to find a comfortable pace.

'Four out and four back, Billy boy?' Walker asked, hoping the cold-eyed Charles might reduce the time magically.

'You gotta pocket watch?' Charles glanced across at his partner.

'Nope. You know I lost my watch in that game of stud two months back. Why?' Walker's face still seemed tense as he jogged up and down in his saddle alongside Charles.

'I ain't got me a watch either.' Billy Charles cleared his throat. 'Reckon we will have to be real careful we don't get it wrong, Duke. I'd hate to find us stuck out here when the sun rises.'

'Shut the heck up, Billy,' Walker snapped, feeling his nerves beginning to play him up once more.

'Just stick close,' Charles muttered.

'And you can stop running off at the mouth for a while, boy.'

Both riders continued aiming their horses straight along the trail left by Ward Jackson hours earlier. They were soon to discover that time itself was meaningless in this strange land they had defiantly entered. Here, the rules of nature became confused and often redundant. Only courage and faith in one's own ability mattered.

This was no place for pocket-watches or those who allowed such devices to control them. This place required much more to satisfy its cravings.

FIVE

Ward Jackson had not allowed thirst or weariness to stop his slow determined advance. He had continued walking onward with his faithful grey mount in tow even after darkness had overwhelmed the vast desert. A million stars and a large glowing moon now replaced the blazing sun but it grew cooler far more slowly than he liked. The sand's heat still penetrated his boots but at least now his skin was no longer being burned from his bones.

Whatever Jackson thought he had seen as he watered the grey for the second time, hours earlier, had still been masked in the sickening vapours of hot liquid air. Yet for the briefest of moments, his eyes had penetrated the illusion and seen the high mesa. Or what appeared to be a mesa.

It had been unlike any other mesa he had encountered over the many years of his wandering across the West. Jackson felt that what his sore eyes had focused upon was not really a natural mesa but something made by the hand of man.

Could it be true? Or had he been delirious due to the torturous heat? Whatever the actual truth, the fleeting image had soon evaporated from his burning eyes when the heat overcame him once more.

Whatever it actually was, it had sure looked like a mesa.

Out here in the desert, it would seem rational to find such a natural monolith, but Jackson knew what he had briefly focused upon was no natural object.

He was almost certain he had seen something that was either carved or constructed to resemble a natural mesa but with each passing beat of his heart, doubts slowly crept into his fevered brain.

Staggering onward through the soft sand in the moonlight, leading the horse behind him, Ward Jackson aimed his every step at the huge black silhouette which towered over him in the distance. With the moon behind the curious stone, a shadow was cast over the sand which appeared to have remained untouched for an eternity.

35

Was he insane, Jackson wondered.

Had the desert just played another trick on him all those hours back? Had it created yet another illusion to keep him heading further and further into a place from where there was no hope of ever returning?

If it were a mere trick, who could have manufactured it?

And why?

As total heat exhaustion finally enveloped his fevered brain and dehydrated body, the simple matter of placing one foot in front of the other became more than he seemed capable of. Jackson felt his head spinning.

Still clutching the reins of his grey, Ward Jackson fell on to his knees as he tried desperately to regain a strength left far behind him in the cruel sand. Even now, an hour after sunset, the sand was still warm and waiting to claim him. He could feel it as its grains trickled through his peeling fingers.

He wanted to close his eyes and sleep. To escape this hell he had so blindly and confidently entered. His heart pounded inside his chest as if warning him not to close his eyes. Not even for the briefest of moments. Although his head was filled with a fog he did not recognize, he knew he had to remain awake. There was only one sleep out here, the sleep of death.

Somehow the emaciated Jackson managed to haul himself back on to his feet using his reins to steady himself. For minutes he just clung to the bridle of his old horse trying to find yet another second wind. As he rested his face against the neck of the proud animal, he knew this unearthly place was getting the upper hand.

'Thirsty, old fella?' Jackson sighed into the animal's ear before moving unsteadily toward his saddle and the canteens hanging beneath his coat.

Checking the canteens in turn he found the fourth and last full one before plucking it off the saddle horn.

His fingers felt numb as he slowly unscrewed the stopper; he leaned for support against the quiet grey horse. It seemed to take for ever to free the stopper of his last canteen. He knew he had to be extra careful, though, as he could not afford to spill even one droplet of its precious contents.

This time it was Jackson who took the first drink. A long, much-needed drink. The water was warm but tasted better than any expensive whisky to his cracked lips and dry throat. Blinking hard, he managed to feel some life coming back to his exhausted body as the water reached its mark.

'This is it, old-timer. The last canteen,' Jackson gasped, as he dropped his hat down on to the ground and carefully poured half of the canteen's contents into it. He watched as the grey lowered its head and began drinking.

Holding the canteen in his hands Jackson gazed out at the high dark object that had lured him this far. Even the moon seemed unwilling to cast its light upon the monstrous edifice. Was it real? Its long shadow was now only a mere ten feet ahead of where he stood. The strange mesa simply had to be real. Even in his confused condition, Jackson knew only reality itself cast a shadow.

He took another mouthful of water, savouring its flavour as he felt it slowly running down into his parched body. It began to dawn on him that he had kept his horse well watered but had almost killed himself by not taking his fair share of the life-saving liquid. Nothing out here could survive long on only sips of water. He had been taught a valuable lesson.

Jackson untied his bandanna from around his head and rubbed the salt and peeling skin off his face as he thought long and hard with a brain which was somehow beginning to function again. He recalled how the sun had been burning down upon the golden medallion which had hung around his neck for over five years and how he had torn it off and thrown it away. He had won it fair and square in a card game long ago. For those five years he had proudly sported the heavy chunk of gold on its thick chain around his neck but as he had been riding across the sun-baked desert he began to see the medallion for what it truly was. A pointless trophy which did nothing except attract the heat of the sun like a naked flame attracts a moth.

Jackson touched his still-blistered skin and spat at the sand. Out here only one thing was vauable and it was the one thing he was now running short of: water.

Was it possible to reach the great black mesa before sunrise, Jackson wondered. Did he have enough water left to get there before the cruel sun reappeared with the dawn?

Could there be life beyond this desert or had he reached the end of the world? So many questions and so few answers.

Looking into the eyes of his grey horse he knew at last what he had to do. Perhaps it was his own reflection which he saw in the placid eyes of the quiet animal, or it might just have been the creature's trusting soul he saw. Either way, he had made his decision and there was no turning back.

He felt a renewed confidence overwhelming

him. Now it was time to do something foolhardy. Something which might prove fatal to the horse, himself or them both.

Jackson knew it might just work. Riding as hard as he could to the distant mesa whilst darkness still ruled this land would tax them both to breaking point, but it had to be his only chance of living to see the sun rising. Now as his strength was on the rise once more, he would give it his all.

He scooped up his hat off the ground, replaced it on his head and felt the soothing droplets of water trickling down his face and neck. If there was water to be found anywhere in this unforgiving landscape it had to be straight ahead beneath the foot of the towering mesa, he assumed.

They had gambled many times over the years and always managed to pull through in one piece. The rider knew his mount was as rested as it was ever going to get.

Time was against them, though. They had six hours at best before dawn. Dawn in this place was a death sentence waiting to be executed and Jackson knew it. He could not take another day out here in this desert.

He replaced the stopper on the neck of the canteen and shook it beside his ear. He heard the sound which he knew was all there was between him and death. That sound of water as it hit the sides of the canteen was all there was.

He stepped into his stirrup, pulled himself up into his saddle and gathered up his loose reins as he looped the canteen strap over the saddle horn.

'Come on, old-timer. Let's give it one last shot,' Jackson said, jabbing his spurs into the flesh of the grey. The horse snorted and began to trot toward the dark menacing mesa. The sand felt strange beneath the hoofs of the grey as it managed to gather pace. Jackson stood in his stirrups and leaned as far forward as he dared, trying to take his weight off the poor creature's back.

The rider was amazed at the courage the old horse showed as it seemed to sense the deadly situation they were in. Faster and faster the hoofs ate up the sand beneath the charging grey animal as it seemed to find unexpected reserves of energy.

Holding tightly on to his reins and balancing himself in a way he thought must be verging on suicide, Jackson caught the scent of something on the air. Then it dawned upon him what was luring the old grey on against all odds. It was the subtle but distinctive aroma of life. Somewhere out there, there was water.

SIX

Billy Charles pulled his reins up short and stopped his horse as his partner slowed to a halt beside him. Walker stared at the young face bathed in moonlight as it just stared directly ahead of them into the sand.

'What's wrong, Billy boy?' Duke Walker asked as he watched his friend dismounting and taking a few steps ahead of their horses. The younger man did not answer as he hovered over the churned-up sand, apparently mesmerized by what his keen eyes had spotted.

Billy Charles bent down and plucked something off the sand before turning and ambling back towards his partner, who sat watching his every action.

'Look at this,' Charles said, holding out something in his hand.

'What is it?' Walker asked as he rubbed his eyes with his bandanna and bent over in his saddle. 'What ya got there?'

Billy Charles raised his arm higher and showed what he had in the palm of his hand. Even in moonlight it was obvious what the gleaming object was.

'A medallion?' The older man gasped as the moonlight danced off its polished surface.

'Not just any medallion, Duke. Jackson's medallion,' Charles corrected.

'So?' Walker shrugged as he vainly tried to see their prey out in the distance.

'It's solid gold, Duke.' Charles rubbed the object on his sleeve as if trying to enhance its brilliance.

'Our first profit in weeks,' Walker said, pulling out his tobacco-stick and biting off a large chunk. 'We oughta quit now and head back.'

Charles pushed the golden medallion into his jeans pocket before getting back on to his waiting horse. He was now feeling confident that they were closer to Jackson than they could possibly have imagined. If the quiet rider was close, so was their money.

'He was wearing this medallion when he beat us at cards, Duke. Remember?' Charles said happily.

'Nope. All I remember about Jackson was he had a gun in his hand trained on us both,' Walker replied before spitting out a large lump of black goo on the sand between them. 'That chunk of gold don't take nothing away from that simple fact, boy.'

'The sun must have baked Jackson's wits clean out of his head, Duke.' Billy Charles grinned broadly. 'I bet he's lying out there foaming at the mouth like a mad dog.'

'How long do you figure we've been riding already?' Walker asked nervously as he stared up at the stars and toward the moon. He had no intention of being caught out here when the sun rose but was reluctant to leave Charles to go on alone.

'Quit worrying about the time, Duke,' Charles laughed. 'I figure we are close to collecting our goods. We can't just quit when we are so close.'

'How come you figure Jackson is close, Billy?' Walker was still troubled as he looked about them at the lifeless blue landscape. 'He might have lost that damn medallion eight or more hours back.'

'He's close, Duke. Maybe he's only a mile or two ahead of us.' Charles kicked his horse forward. 'I ain't quitting.'

'You figure he's loco? How come?' Walker

shouted at the younger man as he set off again over the trampled sand.

'He's starting to lose things. Maybe the sun has driven him crazy. All we gotta do is keep riding and I bet we'll find the saddle-bags with our money in them tossed away, just like the medallion.' Charles stood in his stirrups and looked back at the concerned Walker.

'Wish I was as sure as you seem to be.' Walker watched his comrade heading on, pursuing the tracks. 'Jackson didn't strike me as the sort to turn loco.'

'Come on, Duke,' Charles yelled over his shoulder as he forced his horse to increase his speed. 'Another mile and then we'll turn back. OK?'

Walker knew the younger man was too eager. Too damn eager.

'Hold on up, Billy boy!' he yelled.

'Why?' Charles called out over his shoulder.

'What if he just dropped the darn medallion?' Walker shouted as he drew level with his pal.

Charles looked across. 'The chain was broke. It was ripped from his neck. Jackson must have gotten too much sun and tore the darn thing off his neck. Only someone loco throws away gold, Duke.'

As the two horses kept pace with one another the men eyed the distance ahead before Walker called across to his friend.

'We've been riding a long while, Billy. Maybe it's time we turned back.'

'There's time, Duke. There's plenty of time,' Billy Charles responded without looking in Walker's direction. Now all he had eyes for was the horizon which was blurred by the blue light of the moon.

'But if we go too far, we ain't gotta chance of getting back to the forest before the sun comes up, boy.' Duke Walker tried to reason with his partner, but to no avail.

'Quit belly-aching, Duke. Another mile . . .'

Walker looked back. He could no longer see the thousands of trees they had left earlier. Even the light of the large moon failed to touch their branches from here. 'Maybe we've come too far already, Billy.'

Charles's mind was now concentrated upon the churned-up sand they were riding through. Nothing else mattered to him.

Ward Jackson dragged at his reins and slowed the old grey to a trot. He knew the scent of water had caused the horse's small brain to forget he was carrying a heavy load. Now, as his mount strained on the bit, Jackson controlled the animal and forced it to a walk as he stared

46

around the blackness, trying to get some idea of what they were approaching.

At last Jackson came to a stop and sat in his saddle as the horse grunted beneath him. He looked upward at the massive object that loomed above him and still could see nothing but shadow. His neck hairs began to rise as if warning him that he and his horse might not be alone.

Jackson ran his hand down the neck of the distressed creature as he listened. If his eyes were denied anything to focus upon his ears soon located something a short distance ahead.

Jackson allowed the grey to continue walking ahead slowly as he held tightly on to his reins. Then he became aware of what he was listening to. He could hear the distinctive crashing sound of water as it hit rocks from a great height.

The old grey horse slowed and lowered its head. Jackson realized the animal was drinking. He dismounted cautiously and moved deeper into the darkness until he could see the shallow flowing stream before him. Kneeling down, he scooped up a handful of water and tasted it. It was cold and sweet.

Ward Jackson stayed beside the head of his drinking horse and looked back into the desert which appeared so harmless in the light of the moon. He shook his head as if in disbelief that he had finally managed to cross that vast expanse. Yet where was he?

Wherever this place was, it would only be revealed after dawn. Whatever this place was, it had water. Yet it had always been Ward Jackson's experience that where there was water to be found there were usually a lot of other things too. Not all of them good.

He knew he ought to relax yet every sinew of his aching body told him to remain alert. This place still held a million unanswered questions. Yet he was tired. Dog tired.

As the exhausted Jackson sat beside the stream and listened to its soothing babbling and inhaled the cool air which hovered above its surface, he fell into a sleep like no other he had ever experienced.

SEVEN

The two gamblers had been riding their spent mounts for hours. The promised 'one mile further' had turned into nearly a score but still they rode on, Billy Charles always ahead of his reluctant partner. Always he dug his spurs into the flesh of his mount whenever Duke Walker drew level and tried to reason with him; never was he willing to be discouraged from the course he had set himself.

Duke Walker on the other hand had been getting more and more frightened as he watched the stars in the sky above them moving across the heavens. Even without a pocket-watch he knew time was passing by faster than their horses had been galloping. He also knew they had now gone way beyond any possibility of making it back to the safety of the distant forest behind them. Now it was too late. Now he had to keep following the charging Billy Charles as he drove his horse harder and harder through the trail left by their prey, Ward Jackson.

Walker knew they should have stopped, rested and watered their horses several times before now but the obsessed Charles had just continued forcing his mount on relentlessly through the soft endless sand. Like the born follower he was, Walker found himself doing the same. Once he might have been strong enough to argue vigorously with his partner, but he had grown soft over the years of tagging after the sharp-witted Charles. Now Walker was afraid of stopping his horse and risking being left alone out here in the middle of the desert.

For during all the years they had been together, it had always been Billy Charles who made all the decisions. That had suited the older man, until now. Even during the hours of darkness, without the sun burning their skin off their bones, this was still a desert. It held nothing capable of retaining life for even the briefest of periods. Walker knew it but he doubted if his pal did. As Walker trailed Billy Charles's lathered-up mount he wondered whether they were being drawn into another man's game. Was Ward Jackson toying with them?

Maybe the quiet Jackson had known they were dogging his tracks and had deliberately led them out here to die. Walker tried to catch up with his partner once again but then realized his horse was faltering.

'Billy!' Walker yelled out as his mount began to lose its balance and drift drastically off course. Dragging his reins up he felt the weight of the huge animal lunging from one side to another. With every ounce of his fading strength Walker fought with the horse as it stumbled and began rolling. Somehow the bearded rider managed to stay in his saddle but as he saw the ground racing up towards him, he wished he had managed to slip off the back of the doomed creature.

Before Billy Charles could rein in, he heard the crashing sound behind him as his partner's horse fell heavily. The scream which echoed about the silent desert chilled him as at last he halted his own horse and managed to turn the animal around. The sight which met his eyes as he looked back, sent a wave of horror racing through his body.

The massive horse was on its side, kicking one back leg into the air. For a moment Charles could not see his partner but then spotted a hand whose fingers clawed desperately at the sand.

'Duke?' Charles called out as if doubtful whether the man was still capable of answering him.

There was no reply.

Billy Charles kicked his horse and rode back towards the horrific scene before throwing himself down on to the sand and scrambling towards the shaking arm.

Walker was buried beneath the full weight of the fallen horse in the soft sand. Only his fingers moved at the end of the twisted arm which came out from beneath the massive bulk. Charles grabbed the reins and bridle and started pulling with all his might. Only as the young gambler's boots sank into the soft sand and the horse's head gave no resistance did it become obvious that the creature was dead. The rear leg continued kicking out at the air, the nerves in spasm even as death supervened.

'Duke? You OK?' Billy Charles's voice was raised as he vainly tried to drag the horse off his friend.

There was a muffled sound as the arm waved helplessly from under the dead horse.

Charles knew death had not taken the older man yet, but time was running out. No man could survive beneath the weight of such a heavily laden horse for very long. If Walker was not yet crushed he might soon be or smothered by the beast or sand or both.

Turning, the young gambler stared at his horse and bit his lip as his mind raced. Then his eyes focused on the saddle-rope hanging from his saddle horn.

'Hold on, Duke. I've got me an idea.' Charles ran through the disturbed sand to his horse, ripped the rope from his saddle and began unwinding it. He had never used this rope before in the five years it had hung from his saddle horn but now he was grateful he had not discarded it.

Staggering through the sand, Charles tossed the rope over the head and neck of the dead horse before looping it under one of the forelegs and around the horn of the saddle. He was no cowboy but the loop appeared to be well placed as he tightened the knot and dragged the remainder of the forty-foot-long lariat back towards his own exhausted horse.

He mounted up and wrapped the tightened rope around his own saddle horn and around his free arm. Then he picked up his reins, leaned back in his saddle and jabbed his spurs into the horse's flesh.

Slowly the horse began to move backwards as Charles forced his boots into his stirrups and arched his body, taking the strain with his own frame. With every step the tired horse made, Charles could see the body of the dead beast moving. Each time he jerked at the reins, his horse snorted as it tried to maintain its own balance in the soft sand. A dozen or more times Charles repeated the simple but taxing movement until the huge lifeless horse's body was pulled off the silent Walker.

Only after seeing the creature falling safely away from his partner did Charles release the rope. He threw his leg over his horse's neck and dropped to the ground before racing back towards the confused scene.

With each stride, Billy Charles felt trepidation washing over him. He had been wrong. He had ignored reason just to try and catch up with the man who had beaten them at cards. Walker had tried to reason with him for hours and he had been too smart to even listen. Now as he reached the deep hole in the sand which resembled a hastily dug grave, he felt guilty.

'You still alive, Duke?' Charles shouted frenziedly at the partly visible figure beneath him.

For a matter of a few seconds which seemed like hours to Charles, there was no response. Then Walker managed to roll his head over and stare up at the man with the moon on his back.

'You darn fool.' Walker spat sand from his

mouth as he slowly tried to move one part of his body after another.

Billy Charles moved cautiously into the deep hole to assist his mumbling partner.

'I thought you was a goner.'

'You darn stupid little fool.' Walker added to his insults as he began to edge gingerly up off the sand he had been crushed into. 'I told ya. Didn't I tell ya?'

'Tell me what, Duke?' Charles asked as he slipped his arms under the armpits of his friend and helped the man get back to his feet.

'We had come too far. The horses needed water and rest but you wouldn't stop.' Walker shook himself as sand fell from every part of his clothing and body.

Charles helped the bigger man up on to the undisturbed sand and knew he deserved every curse-word that Walker might have thrown at him if he had not been too dazed to remember any.

'You were right, Duke. I got kinda carried away, I guess.'

'Now what?' Walker managed to stand unassisted as he gasped, trying to regain his thoughts.

'I figure we head back.' Billy Charles shrugged as he stared down at the twisted carcass of the once trusty horse beside them.

Walker moved slowly across the sand to Charles's horse until he reached the saddle horn and the canteen. He lifted it off the saddle and stood as if weighing the object in his hands.

'What's wrong, Duke?' Charles asked as he stepped next to the quiet man.

'This all the water you got, Billy boy?' Walker asked, looking into the eyes of his pal.

'Yep. Why?' Charles was curious.

'This ain't even a quarter full.' Walker unscrewed the stopper and took a mouthful of the water before handing it to the younger man.

'We still got your canteen,' Charles said as he took a swig of the liquid.

Walker shook his head and pointed. 'Didn't ya see the wet sand, Billy? That dumb critter crushed my canteen when she rolled over.'

Charles's face went grim. 'So this is all we got, huh?'

'Yep.' Walker gave out a huge sigh.

'We better head back to the forest, Duke.'

'There ain't time.' Walker found his chewing-tobacco and blew the sand off it before biting off a chunk.

'What ya mean?'

'We better keep heading the way we've been heading, Billy boy. I figure it's closer than trying to get back to the forest.' Walker pointed ahead at

56

the distant mesa, bathed in blackness.

'But what if there ain't no water there?' Charles began to feel fear overwhelming him for the first time since they had started on this futile quest.

'Then we'll die, partner.' Walker screwed the stopper back on to the canteen and hung it back on the saddle.

EIGHT

For the better part of a month the solitary wagon had been heading west deeper into the desert. The three outriders wore their uniforms with less enthusiasm now than when their long journey had begun. Now they wondered when their mission would end. For six months it had been an uneventful expedition into the unknown; then it all changed.

Sent from Fort Sherrington seven months earlier to map the as yet undiscovered boundaries of the southern states, Captain Joel Turner had seen his troop dwindle down to three from the original eight. Leading the trio, Turner held little faith in his remaining riders.

Only the stout wagon-driver, Corporal Sam Hyde, could be relied upon if danger loomed once more. Turner knew Hyde was the only trooper it was safe to turn one's back on.

Running foul of an ill-tempered hunting party of Comanche fifty miles north had seen the small band reduced to the pitiful band they now were. For days the wagon and its three troopers had been chased until they had found themselves driven into this arid desert. Only when they had headed across the burning sand did the Comanche warriors cease their chasing, content that nature would finish the job they had started.

Turner glanced through the moonlight at the small-eyed trooper called Fred White. This was a man who could use his carbine skilfully but was not a man the captain had ever considered real army. There was a dark side to White. He took orders with a silence that troubled the officer.

Riding directly opposite Fred White, Clem Dubony was another trooper who had given Turner more than a little apprehension over the past half-year. Seldom speaking to anyone apart from White the dark-haired man with long crooked teeth nursed his rifle at all times in the crook of his arm. Dubony too had proven himself a fearsome fighter when the troop had encountered the Comanche but seemed to enjoy killing a little more than the captain thought healthy.

Inside the wagon, behind, the large figure of

Sam Hyde, map-maker Byron Gregory sat on a flour barrel. Gregory had somehow managed to survive the vicious battle but had become a virtual recluse in the confines of the cramped prairie schooner. Without him, the mission was over and Gregory was well aware of his own importance. A dozen detailed maps and scores of drawings backed up by photographic glass plates filled the wagon boot-box whilst his tools and equipment lay side by side with their vital provisions. He knew his sheer expertise and meticulous endeavour would assure him his place in history. For countless generations his work would be studied by people as yet unborn. If he were able to survive and manage to take his laborious work back to civilization, that is.

Now even the man born in Boston forty summers earlier began to wonder when this perilous expedition might end. Having come face to face with the Comanche, Gregory wanted no more of this.

Yet he was in the same boat as the four soldiers, forced to head into this arid lifeless landscape by a band of angry Indians who had claimed the lives of five of their original troop.

Gregory peered over the broad shoulder of Sam Hyde and stared out at the three riders leading them deeper into the vast desert.

'Does the captain have any idea where we might locate water, Corporal?' Byron Gregory asked.

'If there's water out there, Mr Gregory, the captain will find it,' Hyde replied, never taking his eyes off the three men leading their way into the strange moonlit desert.

As if hearing the voices on the still night air, Turner pulled at his reins and waited for the wagon to catch him up before allowing his mount to continue beside the driver.

'Anything wrong, Sam?' Turner asked the large man.

'No, sir. Mr Gregory was just asking if we are gonna find us some water in this desert,' the corporal answered.

'See that mesa, Mr Gregory?' Turner pointed with his white gauntlet.

Byron Gregory raised himself up and leaned on the back of the driver's seat, staring to where the officer was indicating.

'Is there water there, Captain Turner?'

Turner pushed his white hat up on his weathered brow.

'I sure hope so. I figure it's our best bet. It also happens to be our only bet.'

Hyde leaned down toward his superior who was riding close to the front wheel of the wagon.

'I don't like the way Clem and Fred have been acting the last couple of days, Captain,' the large corporal muttered. 'Reckon if we hits trouble again that pair of roosters will hightail it out of here faster than spit.'

Turner nodded in agreement. 'I know what you mean but it might just be this damn desert making them a little ornery, Sam.'

'Maybe. Either way I'm keeping both eyes on them just in case,' the wagon driver said as he steered his four-horse team on across the sand.

Gregory leaned further forward and gripped the shoulder of the big driver.

'What's wrong, man?' he asked fearfully.

'Nothing for you to fret about, Mr Gregory,' Turner said as he spurred his horse and returned to the point position of the small troop.

'Could there be more Indians at the mesa, Corporal?' Gregory heard himself ask as he thought about the two troopers who were causing Hyde and Turner concern.

'Not Comanche, Mr Gregory,' Hyde replied quickly.

'If not Comanche, what?' The map-maker felt his entire body beginning to shake as he recalled the sight of the Indians who had fought so determinedly with the troopers only a few days earlier.

'Ain't got no idea what kinda Indians might be

lurking down yonder, sir,' Sam Hyde said honestly.

'Oh dear,' Byron Gregory croaked.

Sam Hyde gave a glance at the map-maker. 'Get some shut-eye, Mr Gregory. With any luck we'll reach that mesa before dawn.'

Byron Gregory sat back inside the rocking wagon interior against the flour sack and felt decidedly uneasy at what he had heard. He knew he was tired but for some reason did not think it wise to go to sleep.

NINE

Suddenly it seemed as if the brash Billy Charles had lost every ounce of his once boundless self-confidence. Now it was the older, more mature, Duke Walker who was calling the shots. For some reason he seemed able to face probable death far more easily than his younger partner. His years before he had met Charles held him in good stead for this type of situation. Walker had skimmed the very jaws of death for most of his adult life until he had hooked up with the clever Billy Charles. It had been Charles who had taught him how to cheat.

But cheating had no place here. This was a problem which had to be faced honestly. Straight on.

Walker had once been a man who had been

capable of thinking for himself and now as he found himself in a dilemma he would rather have avoided, he felt as if he had shed twenty years. Now he had to find the cunning which had served him so well in the past. A cunning which his partner had never mastered.

'What we gonna do, Duke?' Charles repeated for the umpteenth time as he stared wide-eyed out into the darkness at a moonlit desert waiting for them to make a fatal mistake.

'Easy, Billy boy,' Walker said strongly, as he weighed up their options. It did not take very long.

'I reckon we've had it,' Charles muttered as he circled the tired horse waiting for the older man to speak again.

Walker held out a hand and pressed it into the chest of his aimless friend. Their eyes locked. 'Easy, kid. It ain't over 'til I says it's over.'

'What ya blabbing about?' Charles had never seen his partner being forceful before and it came as a shock.

'We ain't finished just yet, boy,' Walker said as he spat out another lump of brown spittle.

'As good as.' Charles's shaking voice could not disguise his total inability to see anything but his own stupidity in leading them here. Now it was he who was fearing the new day and the deadly blazing sun he knew would rise and destroy them.

'We still got a horse. We still got a little water and we are still alive.' Duke Walker knew he had to be positive until his partner regained his normal brashness. Yet this was not like a game of poker; this had a reality about it which Charles seemed unable to fathom.

'How far is it to that mesa anyway?' Billy Charles felt sweat running down his spine as he asked the simple question. He was far from hot and yet the sweat kept on coming. Fear had gripped him the way it had gripped Walker earlier. Now it seemed as if the older man was actually relishing their predicament and it confused the youthful gambler.

'We ran our horses into the ground but at least it means we cut down the distance between us and that mesa,' Walker said calmly, moving ahead to the tracks left hours earlier by Ward Jackson.

'What ya looking at, Duke?' Billy Charles was curious as he followed the older man who was now staring down at the sand and its tracks the way he had when he found the discarded medallion.

'You got eyes. Look!' Walker waved his arm and pointed at the sand at their feet.

Charles did as he was told and then saw what Walker meant.

'Footprints.'

'Yep. Jackson was on foot for most of the way, leading his old horse. That means we must have gained a lotta ground on him by now.' Duke Walker found himself smiling as he spat a lump of black spit straight into the centre of one of the footprints.

'Is that good?' Charles was unsure.

'Maybe not. All I know for sure is there's a chance we can make it off this desert. We ain't beat yet.' Walker stared up at the sky.

'How long we got before sunrise, Duke?' Charles swallowed deeply as he spoke, his eyes never leaving the larger man for even an instant.

Walker shrugged. 'A while. Maybe a few hours, maybe less.'

'I'm sorry I got you into this mess, Duke.' Billy Charles knew he had led them into a death-trap because of his own single-mindedness.

'Reckon we'll walk your horse for a tad,' Walker nodded. 'It must be a good idea, 'cos Jackson did it.'

'I said I'm sorry, Duke,' Charles repeated himself loudly.

'I heard ya, Billy boy. I heard ya.' Walker spat at the sand he detested so much as he moved to the horse. There was a look of determination in the old eyes which seemed alien to the younger gambler.

'Well?'

'I already told ya you're a fool,' Walker said. 'You got me from under my horse though. Reckon we are all square.'

Billy Charles pulled out his tobacco-pouch from his vest pocket and began making a cigarette with unsteady hands and trembling fingers. It was now Walker's turn to make mistakes, he thought.

Duke Walker picked up the reins of the tired horse and began marching off in the direction of the long black shadow which traced across the sand toward them. Billy Charles struck a match and brought it to the tip of his cigarette before shaking his head and following.

TEN

Ward Jackson opened his eyes before truly awakening from the deepest of sleeps. It was no longer dark and the sun was beginning to creep its way into a new day. The air was fresh and sweet as it swept across the stream into his nostrils. Water vapour soothed his skin as he moved up on to his elbows and looked around the lush scenery. It was as if he had awoken into paradise after falling asleep in hell. He had discovered a living world where none should exist. As he lay beside his refreshed horse, staring straight up at the stone monolith, Jackson became aware of sound echoing off the rocks. For a moment he thought it was just the sound of the water as it lashed off rocks in the stream, then he recognized the noise as being something far more serious.

Slowly Jackson began to realize this had been

what had awoken him, this haunting sound which hung on the morning air like an eagle hovering on a warm thermal of air.

Narrowing his eyes, he looked up. Far above him, standing out upon a precarious ledge half-way up the massive rock-face, a lone Indian chanted at the clouds and sky, throwing ground cornmeal into the air. It was as if the half-naked Indian brave was calling to his gods for their blessings, his vocal tones totally in harmony with nature itself.

Although Jackson had never seen one before, he had heard tell of the Pueblo Indians who lived in the high mesas beyond the merciless desert, and of their strange rites. So many stories had passed his way over the years as he wandered ever onward seeking his destiny. Yet for some reason he thought these people had disappeared as so many other vulnerable tribes had done since the white man had ventured, deeper and deeper, into their lands.

To see this thin dark-skinned man with his braided black hair and the solitary eagle feather woven to the crown of his noble head, calling out to the elements, made Jackson regret having found this place.

Had he violated something sacred? Ward Jackson hoped not.

For more than thirty minutes the Indian continued his chanting. Then suddenly he stopped, and clenched both his fists as he looked far off into the desert where the morning sun began to creep across its white surface.

Jackson moved slowly towards a tall lush tree which had had the wisdom to sink its roots deep into the noisy stream behind him. Reaching over to his reins he gently encouraged the now refreshed horse to his side before looking back up at the half-naked Pueblo brave.

Whatever the keen-eyed warrior had seen out on the barren desert had made him rush back into a secret cave far above the watching Jackson.

Ward Jackson rubbed his face as he wondered where the red-skinned brave had disappeared to and what had caused him so much alarm. Turning to take a closer look at the place where he had spent the long night he wondered how such a contrast to the desert were possible. The stream came from a waterfall of more than thirty feet in height.

The entire area around the cold constant water was lush and green. Trees were dotted about at regular intervals, feeding off the fresh water which came from somewhere high above. He noted a small trail which led up through the brush and hugged the very edge of the waterfall. Could that be where he should go? he mused.

Was there something up there waiting to be discovered by a lone traveller?

Jackson thought about the chanting Indian on the rocky eminence, and wondered how many others there might be living hidden from the world around this strange place. Would they take kindly to his entering their private world? He doubted it.

White men meant destruction to these people and Jackson knew that whatever secrets or wonders he might find up there, he would have to take them with him to his grave.

He stepped back a few paces and looked back up at the mesa. Then he saw it, the reason he had thought this was a man-made structure. It made his jaw drop in awe.

More than a hundred feet directly above where Jackson was standing, stretching off into the distance, were adobe-brick buildings filling a massive natural fault in the face of the immense rock. This place could indeed appear to be carved, from out there in the desert, he thought. This was what he had seen through the heat haze.

As his eyes studied the seemingly empty adobes high above him, he began to marvel at their sophisticated design before the hairs on his neck once again began to tingle.

As Jackson turned, he was confronted by the sight of two men leading one horse coming towards him. They were following the tracks he had left in the soft sand hours earlier. Neither man was smiling and both held their weaponry in hands which shook through a mixture of exhaustion and dehydration.

'Put 'em up, Jackson,' Billy Charles ordered as he moved into the shade of the trees beside the grim Walker.

Slowly Ward Jackson raised his arms as he stared straight at the pair of gamblers he thought he had left far behind him in one of the nameless towns he had drifted through.

'Charles and Walker.' Jackson said their names in a low drawl which gave no hint of his emotions.

'Correct,' the bearded man gruffed as he stooped beside their drinking horse and cupped a handful of water up from the stream and into his dry mouth.

'You were lucky,' Jackson said as he looked at the still low sun whose rays continued crawling across the desert as it made its slow journey into the blue sky.

'You figure we was lucky? How come?' Billy Charles tossed the canteen to his partner to fill as he aimed his pistol at Jackson's middle.

'You made it here before the sun got high enough to kill you.'

'It's already damn hot, old man.' Duke Walker passed the full canteen to the younger man and watched as he drank lustily.

Jackson looked upwards briefly before returning his gaze to the two weary gamblers.

'It can get a lot hotter, boys.'

'By the look on your face, I reckon it sure can.' Charles began to smile as he watched the poker-faced man.

'Why the guns?' Jackson raised an eyebrow as he stared straight at them. 'I don't see why you need to train them irons on me. I ain't gonna shoot you.'

'You drew on us the last time we met, Jackson,' Charles said, handing the canteen back to his partner.

'I recall you both aimed to shoot me, Charles.' Jackson glanced up at the adobes again before looking back at the two worn-out men.

'What you looking at up there, Jackson?' Walker asked as he dropped back on to one knee and began filling his canteen again.

'Maybe he's trying to remember how to pray, Duke,' Charles laughed.

'I wouldn't make too much noise around here,

Charles,' Ward Jackson advised. 'This place ain't healthy for the likes of us.'

'Why not, old man?'

'Indians.' Jackson said the word quickly and waited for the reaction it had on their faces.

The faces of both gamblers went serious as they digested the simple word. Neither man had had much experience with Indians and it showed.

'Indians?' Charles began to look upward as the word fell from his lips. Then his eyes saw the strange sight of the adobe dwellings filling the natural ledge of the mesa wall. 'Look, Duke. Look up there.'

Walker squinted and studied the eerie sight.

'What kinda Indians build houses up in the sky, Jackson?'

'I heard tell once of a tribe called the Pueblo,' Jackson answered. 'They like living up in the sky so folks like us can't creep up on them.'

'There ain't nobody living up there now,' Walker announced to his younger companion. 'Them houses have been empty for maybe a hundred years.'

Jackson shook his head. 'I just seen one of them Indians up on that ledge chanting to his gods, Walker. Where there's one Indian I reckon it's a fair bet you'll find a few others.'

Billy Charles edged closer to the side of his

partner as he began to wonder if Jackson was telling the truth or just exercising his ability to bluff once more.

'I remember how you can bluff pretty good when there's a big enough pot on the table, Jackson.'

'That was poker. This ain't poker,' Jackson said bluntly.

'He's bluffing us again, Billy boy.' Walker sighed as he swilled his mouth with cold water again.

'You look scared, boys,' Jackson said.

'Quit fooling.' Walker waved his gun angrily at the man who stood holding his arms in the air.

'I ain't fooling, Walker,' Jackson drawled.

'You ain't?' Charles continued staring up at the strange dwellings high on the rock-face.

'Wish I was. We might be in a heap of trouble.' Jackson shook his head as he started to move towards the two nervous men. As Duke Walker raised his pistol at arm's length and aimed it straight at Jackson's face, he stopped in his tracks.

There was a long silence as the three men stared each other out looking for weaknesses.

The covered wagon and its three army outriders were a mere two miles away from the towering

mesa when Captain Joel Turner raised an arm
and halted their advance. The face of the experienced cavalry officer grew grim as he studied the
mesa which seemed to protrude out of the otherwise flat landscape in an almost unreal manner.
But it was not the sheer magnificence of the rock-
face as the sun rippled across its twisting surface
which attracted the attention of Turner, it was
something else. Something which dried his
throat even more than the ever-increasing heat.

'What's wrong, Captain?' Clem Dubony asked
as he turned his mount and rode up to the tired
officer.

'Look ahead, trooper,' Turner said as he stared
out into the desert at the mesa which loomed out
of the flat sand like a long tombstone.

The trooper raised a hand to his eyes against
the low sun.

'I don't see nothing.'

'Do you see anything, White?' Turner called
across to the other rider who was squinting into
the almost blinding light.

'Nope. It's too bright,' came the simple reply.

Turner dragged his reins and rode back to the
wagon where Sam Hyde sat watching the situation.

'Do you see anything, Corporal?'

Hyde pulled the brim of his hat down to shield

his eyes and looked long and hard out in the direction of the mesa for several seconds before he spoke.

'I thought I did when you reined up but now I can't see nothing at all,' Hyde answered flatly.

'What was it you thought you saw, Sam?' Captain Turner asked in a hushed tone designed not to alarm the sleeping Byron Gregory.

'Smoke, Captain.'

Turner nodded. 'Yep. Smoke. That's what I thought I saw out there on the east ridge. A thin line of smoke rising.'

'Could there be Indians out here in this desert?' Hyde asked the captain.

'Could be Apache. They don't mind the sun however hot it gets, Sam.' Turner removed one of his gauntlets and rubbed the sand from his face.

'Apache don't usually make smoke signals, do they?' Hyde watched the two other troopers ahead of them as they circled their horses waiting for the small expedition to continue.

'Maybe it wasn't a smoke signal. Maybe someone was putting out a camp-fire up there.' Turner leaned across to the water barrel, lifted the lid and stared down into the empty wooden vessel.

'White men this far south?' Hyde tried to reason out the situation using his twenty years experience in the cavalry.

78

'Indians make fires to cook as well as white men, Sam.' The face of the captain was grim as he returned the lid to their empty barrel and steered his horse back beside the wagon driver.

'What we gonna do now, Captain?' Sam Hyde knew they had no choice, but was one of that breed of souls who felt military officers had the ability to work miracles.

'We ain't got much option, Sam. We're out of water.' Turner replaced his gauntlet and gathered up his reins. 'I'm thirsty and that's the only place where we might find some.'

Sam Hyde stared out once more at the mesa bathed in the morning glow of sunlight, and began nodding. He looked down into the face of Turner and spoke with a wisdom earned by over two decades fighting the diverse elements of this vast continent.

'I figure there's water out there, Captain,' he announced.

'You think so?' Turner looked straight up at the big man who held on to the thick heavy leather reins of his team.

'There's clouds hanging over that mesa. Where there's clouds, you nearly always find water, Captain,' Hyde said knowingly.

'And where you find water . . .' Turner began.

'You tend to find Indians,' Hyde completed the

sentence before looking at his superior.

'Yep. That's about it, Sam.' Turner rode back to the waiting White and Dubony before waving them on. Slowly the three saddle-weary riders escorted the slow wagon once again on its perilous journey toward the mysterious mesa.

It was just possible that Captain Joel Turner was leading his small band of followers into certain death, but he knew he had no alternative. They had to try and locate water for themselves and their horses before the sun grew even higher in the morning sky and before it began to burn the flesh from their weary bones once again.

Somehow they had to ignore their fears.

Without being ordered, the two mounted troopers and the keen wagon driver cocked and readied their carbines. Even Captain Turner checked his pistol before returning it to its black leather holster beneath its weather flap. This time however the wary officer did not snap the brass stud home but allowed the flap to remain unsecured.

As the small pitiful expedition began once again to move closer to the strange rock shapes, Turner noticed the thin stream of smoke rising again up into the heavens. Smoke which was a grim warning of a forthcoming doom, yet a warning he could not heed.

ELEVEN

Chief Shatashwa stood amid the mere thirty warriors. This was all that was left of his once prolific tribe's fighting force. Shatashwa carefully watched and listened to the words which passed back and forth across the floor of the cool cave. Of all the voices raised, Talkana the medicine-man spoke the loudest as he urged the meagre band to strike out at the intruders. For Talkana had long envied the Pueblo chief and knew this was his opportunity to gain power. Talkana used words which were designed to fuel the younger braves into acting like real men and not hide in their stronghold with the women. Yet the aged chief allowed the council meeting to continue because he knew that to prevent the cunning medicine-man speaking would do nothing except play into the younger man's hands.

Outside the cave, amid the dozens of adobe dwellings perched high on the mesa wall, women and children waited as they had always done to hear the decision of the council elders.

For decades the Pueblo had farmed the fertile valleys hidden between the high rocks; had lived peacefully in this desolate place with only the occasional interference from passing Apache hunting-parties. Now they had seen the covered wagon and the trio of white-faced bluecoats riding toward them.

Shatashwa had never seen a white man before but his medicine-man Talkana had often warned him of a strange tribe which would one day invade their land and destroy them.

It had been Talkana who had first spotted the approaching invaders and alerted the rest of the tribe. For once, his words had come true and the entire council was worried. But mere worry was not enough for the ambitious Talkana; there had to be blood spilled out on the arid sands.

The blood of the white faces.

Shatashwa paced around his men, never speaking as he listened to their words. The proud chief studied the group and remembered how many strong warriors there had once been, before the fever had come into their mud lodges. How once his two grown sons had stood at his side.

How the fever had taken them and so many others up to the Great Spirit.

Shatashwa had once been a chief with a future but now there were only memories of a kinder past.

The deadly fever had come with the Apache whom they had fought and defeated. Shatashwa feared the invisible enemy more than the physical presence of the new intruders. What diseases did these white-faced men bring to his people? Could he afford to risk contact with them?

Now there were few of his people remaining and he could not face the thought of losing even one more to unseen enemies.

Shatashwa seemed to be the only one within the cool cave who remembered the dangers outsiders brought to their fragile society.

Words of war floated from many of the warriors' mouths as the tension grew inside the cave; words which chilled the old chief as his eyes watched them.

Thirty warriors. A dozen braves who were younger than himself and the rest far older. There had once been more than a hundred strong Pueblo bucks, but no longer. They had all gone to the hunting-grounds in the sky to be with the Great Spirit.

Words of war were coming from the mouths of

men who were afraid because the prophecies of Talkana had seemingly come true.

Chief Shatashwa had sent his wives to the highest point of the great mesa to make a fire and send smoke up into the heavens to warn the white faces away from their land, but they still kept coming. Did these strange white-faced men not understand the messages in the sacred smoke? Shatashwa wondered as he paced.

The voices within the cave were now raised to fever-pitch but the chief still did not speak. He only watched and listened to the ranting of old and young men alike. Talkana was the loudest of all the voices as he raged around in the centre of the seated warriors. This was his moment. He had come of age in the eyes of these men who watched him exercising his rituals.

Yet Shatashwa was unmoved. It had been many moons since he had believed in the magic.

He had no desire to fight these people, whoever they were. To him it seemed that they might simply pass by after watering their animals and never be seen again.

'What does the great Shatashwa think?' the voice of Fetina the elder asked.

'Yes, Great Chief. What do you think?' Talkana screamed from behind his buffalo mask as he leapt about the inner circle of the seated braves.

Shatashwa moved into the centre of his men and bowed his head as he looked each and every man in the eye before speaking.

'I think we should stay here in the high caves until these white-faced men have left our lands.'

His words did not fit the mood of the gathered warriors.

'Do nothing, great Shatashwa?' Talkana came closer to his chief and shook his rattle as he spoke.

'Do you not remember the last time we fought the Apache, medicine-man?' Shatashwa asked.

Talkana raised his thin arms into the air and screamed triumphantly:

'We won a great battle. Did we not?'

'We defeated the foe but then the fever came over our people and destroyed most of our warriors and women and even our children, medicine-man.' Shatashwa shook his head. 'It was the fever from the outside world. The deadliest of all our enemies.'

'These are not stinking Apache. How do you know these men carry the same fever?' Talkana asked forcefully.

'I do not know but then neither do you.' The chief paced around the circle looking into the faces of his men. The older ones began to remember the curse which their victory had brought them. The younger braves seemed unafraid of something they were too young to recall.

'Has our chief become a woman that he will allow strangers to enter our sacred land?' Talkana seemed unwilling to lower his voice as he could tell the younger braves were getting excited by his every word.

'Has Talkana's magic become stronger since our last battle?' The chief watched the medicine-man carefully as he continued to stir the sap of the younger braves who watched his every gesture.

'My magic is stronger. Did I not foretell of the intruders with white faces coming to our land, Shatashwa?' Talkana raised his arms again.

Shatashwa looked at the eyes which hid behind the mask and glared.

'Does your medicine grow stronger than it was when it was unable to save our people from dying?'

'My medicine is strong, Shatashwa,' Talkana said angrily as he strode among the seated braves. 'It was the will of the Great Spirit to take our loved ones to the hunting-grounds in the sky.'

'You are a fool, Talkana.' The chief stared hard at the man who was getting his younger warriors more and more confident with every passing second.

'The Pueblo have never been defeated in battle, Great Chief.'

'There have been too many battles.'

'We must fight to protect what is ours, Shatashwa. It has always been so since the Great Spirit put us here.' The medicine-man moved like a puma among the encircling men.

'You will make many widows this day,' the chief warned.

The medicine-man turned away from the elderly chief and began moving around the warriors, waving his quilled tamping-stick under their noses.

'I will lead you into battle if Shatashwa is afraid. I shall protect you with my magic,' Talkana ranted.

Chief Shatashwa stood motionless, watching the faces of the younger men brighten as the golden tamping-stick touched their black hair in turn.

'You say your magic will protect my warriors, Talkana?' the chief asked loudly, folding his arms.

Talkana turned and nodded. 'My magic will not allow any harm to come to these brave Pueblo warriors, Great Chief. If they follow me into battle they will become heroes as once you were a hero before you grew old and afraid.'

'So be it. Go now to the high valley and get the

ponies we took from our defeated Apache enemies. Ride down into the desert of boiling sand and make war with the white-faced intruders, medicine-man,' Shatashwa commanded with a wave of his arm.

The medicine-man urged the twelve younger Pueblo braves to rise to their feet before rubbing ground cornmeal over their naked chests. Then he moved closer to the stern-faced Pueblo chief.

'We will bring honour to the Pueblo, Great Chief. Victory and scalps to hang from our war lances.'

'Be warned, Talkana,' Chief Shatashwa cautioned the medicine-man. 'If one of these young foolish warriors is killed by the white men, I shall kill you with my bare hands upon your return to the mesa.'

For a moment there was a silence in the cave. Then Talkana led the dozen eager warriors out into the maze of secret valleys to get the Apache ponies.

'Young men always seek the taste of their first blood, Shatashwa,' Fetina the elder said thoughtfully as he rose slowly to his feet with the remaining warriors.

'The taste of blood is always bitter, Fetina,' Shatashwa sighed.

TWELVE

The confused face of Billy Charles went pale as he noticed the smoke signals rising from the stone monolith's highest point above them. The gambler trembled as he found himself unable to take his eyes from the thin twisting plumes of warning smoke drifting up into the heavens. For the first time since being cornered by the two men, Ward Jackson knew at least one of them believed his story about the Indians. The bearded Duke Walker could see the distress in his partner's expression as he placed a solid hand upon Charles's shoulder and shook it roughly until he managed to catch the younger man's attention.

'What's eating you, Billy boy?' Walker asked his physically shaking friend.

'Smoke signals, Duke,' Charles answered. 'Up there on the ridge. Look!'

Walker did look and felt a sudden chill overwhelming him as he realized Jackson had been telling them the truth.

'Oh, sweet Lord. We're goners for sure,' Walker muttered as his fingers gripped the shoulder tightly.

The two men lowered their weapons as they stood open-mouthed opposite the silent Ward Jackson, who was standing with his arms still raised above his head.

'Can I lower my arms now, boys?' Jackson asked the pair of stunned men.

Walker glanced at Jackson and nodded. 'What kinda redskins did ya say these varmints were, Jackson?'

Jackson lowered his arms before turning to stare up at the high mesa. Now he was also scared. Smoke signals meant trouble and he knew that neither of his pursuers was ready for it.

'By the looks of it, they ain't as friendly as I figured they was, Walker.'

'We're in a real fix, Jackson,' Walker said across to the loner who was licking his dry lips as he studied the mesa, trying to see if they had been noticed.

'Just like I said, Walker. We are in a lotta trouble if that smoke means what I think it means,' Jackson drawled.

Billy Charles rushed beside the two men, his eyes wide and glaring as fear raced through his weary mind.

'What the hell we gonna do? Come on, what the hell are we gonna do?'

Jackson looked at the gambler and saw something he did not understand. Fear in itself was a mystery to the man who had survived his last dozen years by forging ahead regardless of obstacles and dangers. To Jackson, the fear he saw gripping the younger of the two men was hazardous to all their health. A man gripped in the jaws of such panic was likely to make mistakes which could cost them dearly.

'Easy, Charles. This kinda problem requires a cool head.'

Billy Charles's eyes flashed angrily. 'You keep that old mouth shut tight or you'll taste lead.'

Duke Walker shook his head as he tried to calm his partner who was still holding his pistol in his unsteady right hand.

'Easy, Billy boy. We might need Jackson's gun skills real soon.'

Charles turned away from both men and returned his fevered attention to the high rockface and the smoke which continued rising defiantly into the blue morning sky.

'How many rounds of ammunition you boys

carrying?' Jackson asked as he once again felt sweat trickling down his face from beneath his hatband.

'Maybe a box of cartridges between us, Jackson,' Walker replied.

'I've got all my shells on my belt and in my pistol,' Ward Jackson told them.

'That's only about twenty rounds at best, Jackson,' Charles exclaimed as panic overcame him.

Ward Jackson looked down into the eyes of the shorter man and nodded.

'Ain't nearly enough, is it?'

Duke Walker rubbed his beard with sweating palms. 'I ain't hankering to mix it with no Indians, Jackson. What do you reckon our best bet is?'

'I figure we might have a chance if we hightail it up through that trail.' Jackson pointed at the trail he had noticed earlier which led up beside the waterfall deep into the lush valleys of the mesa.

'What if that trail just takes us closer to the redskins?' Charles blurted out hysterically.

'If it does we are in one big mess of trouble, Charles.' The voice of Jackson hung on the sweet moist air. 'But if we hang around here I figure we ain't gonna do nothing except die anyways.'

'What the hell are you asking an old man for, Duke?' Billy Charles yelled out at his partner. 'What does he know that we don't?'

Walker leaned over his partner and breathed heavily. 'I told ya to calm down, boy. Screaming ain't gonna do nothing except bring them savages down on our necks faster. Now shut the hell up.'

Ward Jackson said nothing as he watched the two very different men eyeballing one another.

'You ever fought Indians, Jackson?' Walker asked as he tried to work out if there were any other courses of action they might try.

'Ain't even laid eyes on more than a few over the last ten years. Most of them were tame.' Jackson walked slowly across to his horse and removed all four of his canteens before kneeling beside the stream.

'We could kill Jackson right now and take his horse, Duke,' Billy Charles said wildly as he felt his panic growing like a cancer inside him.

Jackson stared across at the two men as he lowered the first of his canteens into the cold water.

'I figure three guns are better than two, Billy,' Walker told his partner. 'Jackson is probably a better shot than either of us, boy. Killing him might just be a suicidal idea.'

'But there's two of us and only two horses.'

Billy Charles added to his idea as a twisted smile etched its way across his face.

'True, but if I'm gonna face a pack of blood-thirsty Indians, I reckon I'd rather like Jackson on my side, Billy boy.' Duke Walker shook his head as he edged closer to the kneeling man filling his canteen.

Jackson handed the full canteen up to the burly man before placing the second empty one into the stream.

'Reckon that smoke is for us?' Walker asked as he secured the stopper of the dripping canteen.

'Can't think who else might be wandering around here. Can you, Walker?' Jackson asked as he kept a keen eye on the disturbed younger gambler behind them.

Billy Charles paced around beneath the heavily leafed tree mumbling to himself. Both Walker and Jackson did not take encouragement from the gambler's display of terror.

'Easy, Billy boy,' Duke Walker called across to the nervous man.

Charles stopped in his tracks and narrowed his crazed eyes as he glared at them.

'I ain't gonna hang around here and get myself scalped for two old bastards like you both.' The words dripped off the tongue of the young man like the venom of a sidewinder.

'Easy, Billy,' Walker repeated as he hung the canteen on to Jackson's saddle horn. 'We are gonna be OK.'

Jackson watched the face of the distressed Charles as he felt the second canteen grow heavy in his wet hand. He had never seen a face so eaten up by fear before. It worried him as he remained kneeling behind Duke Walker's legs. Glancing briefly upwards he noticed the smoke still spiralling into the sky.

'You want me to stay here while you ride off and leave me, Duke?' Charles said waving his pistol angrily at the two men near the stream. 'You figure I'm gonna let you up and leave me here to face them heathen alone?'

'We ain't gonna leave you here, boy,' Duke Walker told the troubled man. 'We'll double up on your horse and let Jackson lead us out of here.'

'What makes you think I'm willing to let you ride with me, old man?' Charles spat at the older man. 'Maybe I would be better off without either of you. Maybe two horses might just get me out of this place in one piece.'

Both Walker and Jackson looked at one another as they soaked up the verbal outburst.

Charles began to laugh. It was not the laugh of a man who had just been told a side-splitting joke, but the laugh of a man whose mind had broken under the strain of events far too fearful for him to accept.

'You take it easy, Billy,' Walker said as he began to realize his partner had lost his reason.

'Oh, Duke.' Charles shook his head as he continued laughing to himself. 'I never thought you was gonna just find yourself a new partner and leave me to the mercy of savages. Ain't it lucky I ain't as dumb as you think I am?'

Duke Walker glanced down at Jackson again with a look of bewilderment carved into his weathered features.

'He's gone a tad loco,' Jackson whispered under his breath to Walker. 'Try and calm him down before he starts using that iron.'

Walker gulped and returned his gaze to the younger man who was now training his pistol on them.

'Hey, Billy. You are just talking a lot of nonsense. Me and old Jackson here ain't gonna leave you.'

'Damn right you ain't.' Billy Charles fanned the hammer of his gun and laughed as his bullets tore through the morning air between them. The first ripped through his horse sending it crashing down beside the old grey, then the second, third, fourth and fifth tore into the flesh of his startled partner.

'What ya wanna go do that for, Billy boy?' Duke Walker asked as he fell forward on to his face. There would be no more questions, only blood and the deafening sound of gunfire as it echoed around the rock-face.

Jackson released the canteen into the water and, withdrew his hand quickly. It was cold and numb as he fumbled for his gun with fingers which seemed unable to respond to his mental commands.

Glancing up through the thick black gunsmoke between them, Jackson saw the laughing man staggering towards him still waving his pistol before him. Charles looked almost drunk as he moved closer and closer. Jackson finally managed to pull his weapon from its holster.

Charles raised the gun and aimed his shaking hand straight at the sweating Jackson.

Cocking the hammer and squeezing the trigger, Billy Charles fired his sixth bullet.

There was a chilling sound behind Jackson's spine as he heard his faithful old grey horse whinnying in agony before falling heavily on to its side.

Ward Jackson rose to his feet holding his gun in his unfeeling hand. The wrinkled eyes looked down at his wounded horse as it lay grunting with the bleeding bullet-hole in its neck, its eyes following his every move. For the first time in all the years he had been travelling, Jackson felt anger.

Stepping over the body of Duke Walker, Jackson walked towards the still laughing man.

'Now there ain't no horses, old man,' Charles grinned as he emptied his gun of spent shells.

Jackson raised his weapon but still could not manage to make his fingers do his bidding.

'I seen crazy before but you take the biscuit, Charles.'

Suddenly there was an ear-splitting humming noise screaming through the air. Then a thud which caused dust to fly off the back of the young gambler. Billy Charles arched his body as the impact threw his body forward.

Ward Jackson stared down in total disbelief at the arrow in the back of Billy Charles, who lay at his feet.

Looking up cautiously, Jackson tried desperately to see where the deadly arrow had come from.

THIRTEEN

It had been a mere ten minutes earlier high up in the hidden valleys of the mighty mesa when the seeds of Billy Charles's fate had been sown. The medicine-man had managed to stir the twelve young Pueblo braves into a fevered frenzy. Using his mastery of his trade, Talkana had convinced the painted warriors that they were invincible because he had bestowed upon them the magic passed down to him over a hundred generations.

The paint which he applied to their dark faces would not allow any harm to befall them whilst they were on this valiant mission. The eagle feathers which he had blessed and tied to each of their war-lances would make the weapons find their chosen targets.

Whether or not Talkana believed his own wild ravings was impossible to tell. Yet as he blessed each of the ponies that his enthusiastic followers were mounting, his manner changed.

Grabbing tightly on to the mane of his pony and throwing himself up on to its bare back, he removed his buffalo-mask and tossed it at the feet of the stone-faced chief.

As their eyes met, the two men from different generations looked coldly at one another. Their mutual hatred bridged the twenty-feet distance between them as the young bucks began to ring out their chilling war chants.

'Behold, Shatashwa. Behold the dawn of a new age for our people. Rejoice in the coming of a new chief and a new age of prosperity for the Pueblo,' Talkana yelled as he pulled his war-lance out of the sand and raised it above his head until the breeze caused the eagle feathers to flutter.

The old chief stepped forward and then folded his arms as he glared up at the excited medicine-man.

'This will not bring a new age for our people, Talkana. This day will see many widows who will curse your name to the heavens for allowing their men to die out there on the white sand.'

'The people of the mesa deserve a chief with fire in his blood to lead them, not an old man whose flame has gone out long ago, Shatashwa,' Talkana snarled down at the grim-faced chief.

The Mysterious Mesa

'You shall never be chief of the Pueblo, medicine-man,' Shatashwa said coldly. 'Enjoy what is left of your day because as I warned you, if one of these braves dies I shall kill you with my bare hands.'

'Big words, old man,' Talkana hissed.

'We shall see who has the greater magic before the sun sets this day, Talkana,' Shatashwa sighed heavily.

Swinging his mount violently around, Talkana kicked his pony hard and clung to its mane as he led the small band of screaming warriors down through the narrow canyon-trail carved between the gigantic rocks of the mesa. He did not hear or heed the warnings of a man he had envied for his entire life. The medicine-man was out to seek glory as a thousand others had done before him through the endless annals of history.

After watching the misguided braves descending to the floor of the desert, Chief Shatashwa turned away from the dust created by their painted ponies and looked into the faces of his faithful warriors. Most, like himself, were old and many moons past their best days. As he walked through them back into the caves which led to the adobes the wise chief did not say anything. There were no words which could express his feelings of total and utter despair.

Shatashwa knew the medicine-man had only one reason for leading the last of his tribe's young men into battle. It was not to protect the Pueblo. It had nothing to do with honouring their gods. Talkana wanted to make his mark in Pueblo history. Self-glorification was the saddest of all sins.

The old chief knew that without their young men his tribe had little chance of creating a new generation; in time there would be no one left upon the great mesa to be taught anything about the once honourable Pueblo.

As all the elders entered the cave behind Shatashwa, only one warrior remained out in the high valley. His name was Chokata. Neither old nor young, the brave with the bow and quiver full of arrows moved up the smooth rock-face with the agility of a mountain goat.

He would do as he had been instructed and wait until he had a target to aim his deadly arrows at. Talkana had told him if he and the young screaming braves managed to chase the white-faced intruders into the small clearing at the foot of the mesa, it was his duty to use his archery skills to kill them one by one from his high vantage-point amid the adobes. Chokata would do as the medicine-man ordered without question because he was the brother of Talkana.

It had been his arrow which had found the spine of the crazed Billy Charles with such ease.

Chokata held one other secret instruction from his ambitious brother within his unfeeling brain. Given half a chance he would save one of his arrows for Chief Shatashwa.

FOURTEEN

The covered wagon was tearing across the white sand towards the mesa. Its team of four emaciated horses responded to the bullwhip which cracked above their heads and the smell of the distant water in their nostrils. Since hearing the gunfire the small cavalry troop had increased its speed.

There was no time to worry about the smoke signals. They had little option but to attempt to find cover before they were caught out upon the flat arid landscape. Captain Joel Turner gritted his teeth as he led his two mounted troopers Dubony and White across the remaining distance and Corporal Sam Hyde used every muscle in his massive arms to force his lathered team to keep up.

Steering his mount alongside the wagon driver, Turner pointed at the greenest point of the mesa, which lay at the foot of the incredibly huge rock structure. Quickly using well-rehearsed signals, the captain made it clear where their chosen destination would be. Hyde nodded his understanding to the officer and dragged his reins over hard to his left so the four horses knew exactly where he wanted them to go. Lashing his thick leather reins down across the backs of the team he urged them on.

Turner returned to the head of the small force and waved both White and Dubony on as he held back in case the wagon and its passenger required protection. Troopers White and Dubony drove their mounts on, leaving the captain and the covered wagon in their wake. It was a calculated decision to allow the pair of riders to find cover ahead of him but Turner had little time to think.

Finding himself upside down in the back of the rocking wagon, map-maker Byron Gregory clawed his way through the array of provisions towards the ample rear of the corporal. It was no way to be awoken from a deep sleep, but at least Gregory was grateful that he could be woken up. It meant he was still alive.

'What's happening?' the map maker screamed

above the noise of the wagon as it groaned under the strain of being thrown about the floor of the desert at high speed.

Hyde glanced at the head which bobbed around behind him before returning his concentration to the task at hand.

'Get ya butt up here next to me, Mr Gregory.'

'What?' Gregory's voice seemed to reach a pitch far beyond a normal man's range as his hands gripped the back of the driver's wooden seat.

'Get up here, man,' Hyde shouted over the sound of his team's pounding hoofs.

Gregory managed to balance himself. 'Why?'

'Look over yonder. We got company,' the corporal spat through the sand-filled air to his left.

Gregory leaned out around the flapping canvas and stared at the sloping land at the side of the gigantic rock. His eyes seemed to double in size as he focused upon the dozen or so half-naked riders who were heading in their direction, carrying shields and feathered lances.

'Indians again.' The map maker's voice choked on the word.

'Yep. Indians. Now get ya ass up here.' Hyde lashed his heavy leather reins up and down across the backs of the team as he drove his wagon after the three riders' dust.

Gregory somehow managed to get his long thin

left leg over the wooden seat and follow it until he found himself sitting next to the big sweat-soaked corporal.

'What do you want me to do, Hyde? I can't drive a four-horse team. I'm of no use in situations like . . .'

Hyde spat again. 'Get my carbine up off the floor and start shooting, Mr Gregory. Just keep shooting.'

Gregory held on to the back of the long wooden seat and reached down into the deep box at their feet. Grabbing at the barrel of the army-issue carbine, he began to manoeuvre himself back up beside the busy driver.

'I'm not much of a shot, Corporal,' Gregory admitted as he wrestled with the long-barrelled weapon.

'Just start shooting, man,' Hyde growled as he saw the Pueblo braves reach the level white sand and begin their frenzied approach towards the fleeing army troop. Hyde raised an arm and cracked his bullwhip above his head keeping the four gallant horses charging through the baking hot air towards the ever rising sun and the indomitable mesa.

'I'm no marksman, Corporal. I'm just a map maker.' Somehow Byron Gregory managed to cock the rifle and fire in the general direction of the charging band of Indians. The violent kick from the carbine pushed him back into the burly cavalryman.

'Keep shooting; them redskins ain't joking. If they get close enough, they'll be hanging our scalps on them war-lances.' Hyde gritted his teeth against the hot burning air as he screwed up his eyes tightly, trying to see through the blinding sun and choking sand.

'They'll scalp us?' Gregory's voice screeched out in blind terror as he clung to the weapon.

'Damn right. Shoot, man. Shoot.'

The thumping pain in his bruised shoulder ignored, Byron Gregory continued cocking the carbine and firing out at the painted warriors who made their spine-chilling cries echo about the desert floor as they rode ever closer. Concentrating on the business of working the army-issue rifle, Gregory had no time to worry about his weak muscles or their colourful attackers.

'That's it. Keep shooting!' Hyde yelled out as he cracked the whip again. 'You might not hit any of them but you just might scare them.'

Byron Gregory heard the fire in the gravel voice of the wagon driver and continued firing. He had never even held a weapon in his hands before, let alone fire one. As he stared down the long barrel through the sight at their attackers, his blood ran cold as he wondered what he might feel should one of his bullets actually find their target.

The sweating map maker did not have to harbour the fleeting thought for long. An arrow drove itself into the side of the wooden seat next to his thigh and caused him to jerk backwards and fire quickly. Through the smoke from his rifle barrel, Byron Gregory watched as one of the Pueblo warriors fell from the Apache pony he had been riding.

'Good shot, man,' Sam Hyde chortled as he drove the team on after Captain Turner's mount.

Gregory felt his confidence rise as he cranked the mechanism of the rifle again. He had tasted the strange flavour of death in his Boston mouth. To his surprise and horror, he liked it.

The captain had seen his men disappearing into the heat haze below the base of the great mesa as he leaned around in his saddle and stared at the thundering wagon behind him. The Indians were gaining quickly on the wagon and its valuable cargo.

Without a second's hesitation he knew exactly what he had to do. Pulling up on his reins and slowing until the four-horse team drew level with his mount, Turner stood in his stirrups and reached up to one of the exposed wagon-bows not covered by the huge canvas and grabbed it with his left white gauntlet. As his horse galloped beside the front wheel of the racing wagon, the captain kicked his boots free of the stirrups and hauled himself up beside Sam Hyde.

Without a word being spoken, Turner scrambled over the back of the long rocking driver's seat and found himself inside the bouncing wagon. He ripped the catch off a long box and pulled out a gleaming unused Spencer seven-shot repeating rifle which had not seen the light of day since leaving the factory eighteen months earlier. Quickly he loaded the weapon and exchanged it for the empty one. He patted the back of Gregory's silk vest.

'You're doing a grand job, Mr Gregory,' Turner said, as he grabbed a handful of cartridges and began loading the weathered rifle still wet from the map maker's sweat.

'I wager a twenty-dollar gold piece I kill another of these savages before you do, Captain Turner,' the excited voice of Byron Gregory called down to the officer.

'You got yourself a bet, Gregory,' Turner said, as he moved to the side of the wagon and knelt down.

Pulling the canvas side of the wagon up a few

feet, Turner pushed the Spencer's long barrel out and trained its sight upon the approaching warriors. His well-educated eyes had never seen this tribe before and he wondered who or what they were as he squeezed off his first shot. None of them had any rifles, he noted. Not even handguns. They had bows and lances. What tribe would attack well-armed soldiers with mere bows?

As his first shot missed by a mile any of his chosen targets he wondered whether it was the continuous bouncing of the wagon which had caused his inaccuracy or the rifle in his hands itself. The Spencer was known for its tendency to misfire or shoot wide of the mark but compared to the single-shot Springfield carbines and rifles, it saved time. With seven bullets in its breech, it sacrificed accuracy to volume and the quick speed of fire gave the less talented soldiers a feeling that they might just hit something as they discharged the seven bullets.

'Damn Spencer rifles,' Turner cursed as he recalled the much greater range of his beloved Springfields. You could keep Indians at bay with a Springfield. Indians got too damn close when you had Spencers. They had only half the range. Why had they been issued with Spencers in the first place? Apart from the battle of Beecher's

Island back in 1868, they had been shunned by nearly all army outposts.

Firing again and again, Turner watched as the screaming warriors grew closer. So close he could see the paint on their faces.

'We're almost there, Captain!' Hyde yelled out in his loudest voice. 'I can smell the water and so can the horses.'

'Thank God,' Turner muttered to himself as he watched their attackers bearing down upon them. Now it was the whites of their eyes he could see as he angrily pulled at the trigger once more without success.

FIFTEEN

Fred White and his fellow trooper Clem Dubony dragged their reins up to their chests as they stopped their mounts at the edge of the cold winding stream. The scene of carnage which met their blistered eyes stunned the two hardened soldiers as they hastily dismounted from their horses and began to run for cover. Dubony fell on his stomach beneath the canopy of the large tree and stared about at the unearthly scene of two dead men and the pair of stricken horses. Then he noticed his companion standing beside the two horses, watching the rock-face. There seemed no fear in the crouching cavalryman.

Fred White took the time to study the high mesa above them as he withdrew his .45 from its holster. Glancing back to his colleague the trooper swallowed deeply as he caught a brief glimpse of the Indian moving above them amid the adobes. Raising his pistol, White fired up into the rocks.

'Keep down, Clem,' White shouted as he pulled the hammer back on his pistol again until it locked into position.

'Indians?' Dubony rolled on to his side and tried to see what his fellow trooper was pointing at above them.

'Yep.' White ran a tongue over his dry lips as he tried to judge whether the Indian was alone or not.

'Get over here fast, Fred, before the darn critter starts shooting at you,' Dubony yelled out as he crawled to the edge of the moving shadows of the trees and squinted upwards.

White crouched and ran from beside the drinking horses as fast as his tired saddle-sore legs could take him. As he leapt over the body of Billy Charles, Fred White heard the unmistakable sound of an arrow leaving an Indian bow. He threw himself on to the ground beside his fellow trooper and crawled next to his waiting companion.

A few seconds later the pain reached his brain. Screaming in agony the soldier raised himself up on to his wrists and looked down at his leg and saw the arrow that had skewered itself half-way

114

through his boot and calf muscle. Although the only blood to be seen covered the flint arrowhead, White could feel his boot filling with his life's precious liquid.

Dubony grabbed his friend's shoulders and steadied the man as he rolled around in the sand screaming.

'Easy, Fred. Let me pull out the arrow,' Dubony shouted trying to bridge the gap between them. A distance of only a few inches and a pain beyond measurement.

'Clem? Help me, Clem!' White called out as he felt his leg being grabbed by the strong hands of Dubony.

For a moment Dubony said nothing as he wrestled his fellow trooper to a standstill by using his superior weight. Then he felt White's body relax beneath him and looked at the blood which was beginning to flow from the boot on to the sand. Looking back at the pale face he could see the shock carved into its tanned features. Fred White could no longer feel anything as pain tore away at his fragile grip on reality.

The army boot concealed the true extent of the horrific injury from Clem Dubony's eyes as he stared at the arrowhead dripping blood into the sand. For a moment he wondered what to do, then he knew there was only one choice.

Carefully and cleanly snapping the tip of the lethal projectile off, the trooper took a long deep breath before pulling the remainder of the wooden shaft out of the jagged wound. Blood squirted with every beat of the man's heart.

Not wasting another second, Dubony pulled the long boot from White's leg to reveal the true extent of the bloodcurdling wound. The blood poured out of the leather on to the sand at the trooper's knees as he desperately tried to stop the bleeding. Dubony had seen many wounds before but none which bled, like this. The bright red liquid seemed to pump out from both the entry and exit wounds as the trooper tried to think of what to do next.

He was no doctor but knew nobody could afford to lose as much blood as this and live. White had only one chance and it rested squarely in Dubony's hands.

Ripping his grubby yellow bandanna from his neck, Clem Dubony wrapped the ragged cloth around the wound and tied it as tightly as he could.

Even this seemed to have no effect. The blood still kept pumping out through the material as if it were not there.

Untying it again, Dubony raised the blood-soaked bandanna up to the knee and then tied it

116

tightly once more. This time he slipped the
broken arrow-shaft into the knot and began turning it tighter and tighter until the blood loss
began to slow to a trickle.

The covered wagon pulled by its team of four
sweating horses ploughed its way into the clearing and only stopped when it reached the cold
waters of the stream. All three of its weary occu-
pants leapt from the arrow-scared vehicle as the
sound of screaming Indians grew louder in the
distance behind them out on the desert plain.

Captain Joel Turner forced Byron Gregory
under the wagon-bed before noticing the two
troopers beneath the canopy of the tree. He
rushed across and slid on to his knees beside his
men, who were covered in the crimson juice of
violent attack.

Turner stared down at the pale-faced Fred
White who lay mumbling as he drifted in and out
of consciousness. Then he saw the makeshift
tourniquet in Dubony's red hands.

'You did a good job there, Clem.'

It was the first time Dubony had heard the
captain call him by his first name and it shook
him even more than the blood-flow which he had
fought with such gallantry.

'There's an Indian up there with a bow, sir.'

Turner glanced across at the body of Billy

117

Charles before returning his attention to the grim trooper.

'Seems to be a damn good shot.'

'He hit Fred on the run,' Dubony added as he tightened the tourniquet an extra half-turn. 'Fred didn't even know he was hit until he reached me.'

'That's darn good shooting with a bow.' Turner looked around in the hanging branches and tried to get a good look at the well-hidden Indian.

'Ain't no use trying to see the varmint, sir. He's moving around up there like a damn ghost.' Dubony sighed heavily. 'I ain't even seen him but I sure seen evidence of his skill at killing.'

'You got two pistols?' Turner asked his man.

'Yep. Fred's and mine,' the trooper answered slowly as he listened to the sound of the Indians growing closer and closer with every passing second.

'Fully loaded?' The officer stared straight into the face of the troubled man. It was the first time he had truly seen the real Clem Dubony.

'Yes, sir.' Dubony nodded again.

'If these hostiles get close, use every round, Clem.' Turner raised himself on to one knee and studied the scene. Corporal Hyde had unhitched the team and driven them into the stream with the other horses whilst instinctively keeping the wagon between himself and the arrows that rained down from the mesa.

Somehow, against all the odds, Sam Hyde managed to join the terrified Gregory beneath the wagon. Only when satisfied his man was safe did Turner take a long overdue breath and concentrate on the two troopers beside him again.

'What we gonna do, Captain?' Dubony asked as he picked up Fred White's pistol with his free hand whilst maintaining his grip on the tourniquet.

'Praying might come in useful just about now,' Turner said honestly.

'I ain't one for praying as a rule, sir, but . . .'

Turner glanced at the younger man and slapped him on the shoulder before heading back to the others.

'You did good here, Clem. Damn good.'

SIXTEEN

Ward Jackson had somehow managed to avoid the deadly arrows which had sought his life from the bow of Chokata. Fleeing up the narrow overgrown trail into a safer place, he had managed to cross over the top of the waterfall unscathed, to safety. Faced with the massive mesa which loomed above him, Jackson wondered how anyone could possibly reach its summit, and yet there was at least one Indian up there. Probably a lot more.

Climbing up through a narrow brush-covered canyon which skimmed the edge of the sheer rock-face, Jackson slowly made his ascent. The tired desperate man who climbed continually upwards was a long way from the confident man who had met the desert face-on less than a day earlier. Now he was without his horse for the first time since he had started out upon his epic quest more than a dozen years earlier. Escaping from the deadly arrows, he had left his precious canteens far below him along with his meagre provisions.

He had saved his own skin but it had cost him dearly. All he had left was the pistol in its holster and half a belt of bullets strapped around his hips. And he faced a near vertical climb.

Clinging to the tall twisting plants which rose from the damp soil around the gigantic rock, Jackson wondered where he was heading. There had been a safer route down across the stream above the rim of the waterfall yet he had never been a man to choose the easy way out of any situation. Wherever this small trail led, he would stick with it to the bitter end. The echoes of screaming Indians and further gunfire echoed off the towering rocks from far below but still he continued climbing.

There was no reason to keep going on but Jackson had lost all his reason long ago when Billy Charles had gone loco and tried to kill everything his gun aimed at. Turning back was no longer an option as the sound of gunfire filled his ears. The route ahead was dangerous but at least there wasn't anyone aiming a gun in his direction.

Twelve years of seeking a destiny which would make his name had disappeared in the acrid stench of Billy Charles's crazed gunsmoke.

Now all that was left reached up into the sky above him like a giant waiting for him to scale its dizzy heights before flicking him off like an unwanted bug.

No longer did the silent man wonder what his destiny might eventually be, only whether he was ever going to survive this place in one piece. If only he had managed to grab one of his canteens when the Indian had started shooting arrows down at him. Ward Jackson's throat was dry again.

Could there be water up there beyond the jagged rock-face?

There had to be water up there, Jackson told himself. It was a thought which drove him on up into the hazardous landscape.

The sound of guns firing below him caused Jackson to hesitate and stare down from his perilous perch. There was nothing to see but the tops of trees from where he rested. Sweat no longer dripped from his tired brow but dried on to his skin like acid as it burned into his flesh. The air was thinner the higher he climbed. Staring around he began to wonder where the Indian with the bow and accurate arrows might be hiding.

For a moment he thought about the lethal accuracy of the Indian who had inadvertently saved his life by killing Billy Charles. Then he remembered how the same Indian had shot three arrows at him before he had managed to reach the safety of the thick brush.

Looking around the desolate scene, Jackson noticed a ledge which was just within reach if he were brave enough to step out into mid-air and put his trust in something bigger than his own self. For a few moments, as the sound of guns firing far below him filled his ears, he hesitated.

Then he moved.

Like a mountain lion, Jackson sprang away from the relative safety of where he was into a void of where he wanted to be.

How he managed to bridge the gap and find a sure footing on the ledge was beyond him, yet he did so. Resting with his face buried against the cold rock-face, Jackson opened his eyes once more.

As he gasped for air, he somehow managed to taste a sweeter flavour hanging on the moist thermal which drifted across the almost flat rocks into his dry mouth.

There was water somewhere close. Jackson could taste it.

A few yards along from where he rested the

sun drenched the surface of the rocks with all the fury he had suffered on the white sandy desert.

Beyond that point was a sky which was vivid blue.

Now he had a six-inch-wide ledge to move his scuffed cowboy boots along until he reached the corner of the near vertical mesa wall. What lay around the mountainous corner, he could only imagine as the shots echoed about him. His ears were filled with the nerve-breaking noise which confused him as he slowly slid one boot sideways before moving the other.

Who could be shooting? he wondered.

Charles was deader than a turkey at Thanksgiving and the poor hapless Walker had more holes in him than a termites' home.

The deadly Indian archer had only a bow. There had to be somebody else down there, Jackson concluded.

But who?

As Jackson felt his belly slide across the rock as he edged ever closer to the acute corner of the wind-smoothed mesa wall he kept thinking about the shots. But no matter how much he thought about it, the answer became no clearer.

Was it possible that other white men had ventured to this strange hostile land?

For him to have crossed the desert, Jackson

mused, was verging on insanity, but when the pair of gamblers had trailed him to the oasis, he had been totally surprised. Now it seemed there were others down there.

Once more the deafening shots rang out as their sound bounced off the rocks around him. Jackson felt his right foot slip off the narrow ledge briefly before he managed to steady himself. He clung to the wall of solid rock shaking in terror as he glanced down at the sheer drop.

Jackson began to feel a renewed strength, and confidence tracing through his body as his bleeding fingers found the edge of the wall of rock. The sky was a blue unlike any he had ever seen before and it seemed as if he were actually close enough to be able to touch it.

Now the corner was only a matter of inches away from the face of the drifter as he felt the heat of the sun begin to fry him in his own sweat once again, as it had done on the desert floor the previous day. What would he find when he reached the edge of the sharp rock-face, he wondered? Would there be level ground or nowhere to go?

Ward Jackson cringed as more shots rang out around him from far below. Each time he heard the gunfire, he shook with terror as he tried to remain attached to the high mesa wall. One false step would be his last.

Jackson's clothing felt as if it were ablaze as he wondered what lay beyond the razor sharp mountain edge. Was he crazy to even be in this place? Had insanity finally swept away all his judgement?

Then the shots rang out again and he hesitated, trying to keep his mind focused on the job at hand. Glancing down at his right boot he could see how little rock he was now standing upon. A mere two inches was all there was between him and a deadly fall into a place he was unable to see.

Was he loco?

If he were, he sure wasn't alone in his madness.

SEVENTEEN

Captain Joel Turner rolled over beside the growling Sam Hyde and fired another shot out from under the wagon at the screaming band of Indians who seemed unable to do anything but continually attack. There was an obsession driving the painted Pueblo warriors which did not seem to the experienced soldiers to have any rhyme or reason to it. Turner had noticed that each time the braves appeared to be seeing sense, one of their party urged them on once again. Unknown to the small expeditionary force was the fact that Talkana the medicine-man had bitten off more than he could chew by attacking the strange white-faced intruders. Having never encountered firearms before, or tasted their lethal bullets, the Pueblo Indians were baffled.

Talkana remembered the words of his chief as

he gathered what was left of his pitiful war party together. He knew Shatashwa would not shy away from his promise and try to kill him for leading so many to their deaths. All the medicine-man could think of was how he might turn this defeat into something which appeared to be a victorious crusade. He desperately needed scalps to hang from his war-lance, yet the strange fire-sticks which had claimed half his band had more magic than he possessed.

As Captain Turner squeezed his trigger once more he saw another of the brave Pueblo falling into the sand. It was too easy, he thought.

'What's eating them, Captain?' Hyde spat to his side as he tried to see through the clouds of dust the galloping ponies had created. 'How come they don't quit?'

Turner emptied his spent shells into the sand and reloaded his trusty Colt again.

'Beats me, Sam. We've killed at least half of them and still they keep attacking. It's as if they've never seen rifles and pistols before.'

'It makes no sense!' Byron Gregory screamed as yet another arrow hit the sand close to the large wheel beside him.

'Stay calm, Mr Gregory,' Turner said as he snapped his pistol back together and cocked its hammer.

'He's right. They ain't even got guns and yet they still keep attacking us.' Kydd felt guilty at taking so many lives due to an unfair advantage.

Turner nodded in agreement. 'I've got to agree, Sam. It turns my guts shooting such inept opposition.'

'I figure we ain't got a lot of rounds left, Captain,' the angry corporal said as he watched the Indians regrouping again just out of range.

'There's plenty of ammunition in the wagon, Sam,' Joel Turner said as he vainly tried to reason out the actions of their attackers.

'We got a half-dozen Indians this side of the wagon and a damn good shot with a bow behind us.' Hyde stared at his superior with a blank look. 'It's suicide to even try and get up into the wagon and you know it.'

Turner nodded as he looked out at the six mounted Indians facing them through the dust. Even now their defiance radiated across the distance between them.

'If necessary, I'll try and get the ammunition myself, Sam.'

Hyde spat at the sand again. 'I'd rather you stayed here with me and Mr Gregory. A dead captain ain't much use to me and the boys.'

Joel Turner smiled and patted the crusty older man on his shoulder.

Suddenly there was a sound which echoed around the small watering area. A sound which caused equal alarm in the mounted warriors and the small scattered expedition force.

'Drums!' Sam Hyde exclaimed as he gripped his Spencer rifle in his large hands.

'What does it mean, Captain?' Gregory asked fearfully.

Turner crawled through the sand to the rear of the wagon and tried to ascertain where the heart-stopping sound was coming from. It was impossible to tell.

'It must be coming from somewhere up there in those mud structures, men,' the officer shouted loudly.

'But what does it mean?' Gregory repeated his question.

'I'm not sure, Gregory,' Turner replied as he saw the half-naked figure of Chokata scrambling away from his deadly vantage point. 'Whatever it means, the Indian with the bow and arrow has hightailed it out of here.'

'Look, Captain.' Gregory raised an arm and pointed out at the white hot desert and what remained of their attackers.

'What is it, Mr Gregory?' Turner asked as he moved back towards the frightened map maker.

'They seem to be departing,' Gregory sighed with

130

relief as his shaking arm lowered back into his lap.

'Good Lord, he's right, Sam,' Turner said as he placed a hand upon the broad shoulder of the corporal. 'I reckon those drums must be some sort of signal for them to retreat.'

'Its about time, Captain.' Hyde sighed heavily as he lowered his head on to his arms.

The three men watched as the Indians rode their ponies away from the bloody scene. Even Talkana knew it was unwise to ignore the drums. Chief Shatashwa had ordered them to return to the great mesa.

'It could be a trap,' Hyde grunted. 'Indians are tricky critters when they have a mind.'

'I doubt it. It must have something to do with the drums, Sam.' Captain Turner looked back at the tree and the two troopers who had remained in the same spot throughout the siege. 'I'd better check on White and Dubony.'

Hyde watched as the determined officer ran crouching across to the pair of stranded troopers. Without even thinking of his own safety, the large corporal crawled out from beneath the wagon and rose to his full height, still clutching his carbine firmly in his hands.

Turner's smile soon evaporated in the morning air as he saw the sight under the branches of the large tree.

'Are you OK, Clem?'

Dubony glanced up from beside his dead companion, still holding the tourniquet in his hand.

'Is it over, sir?' the trooper asked in an almost trance-like voice.

Turner pulled Dubony's blood-covered fingers free of the makeshift bandage and discarded it.

'Fred don't need any more help, Clem.'

'I think he died, sir.' Dubony's voice was hollow.

'He lost too much blood. You did your best.'

Dubony looked about them and then seemed to hear the drums for the first time. His eyes darted around as if trying to locate the drummer. 'What is that, Captain?'

'Don't you pay them drums any mind, Clem,' Turner said, helping the cavalryman on to his feet.

'I ought to bury old Fred, sir.'

'Not yet, Clem. Right now we better try and make sure we manage to remain alive.' Turner leaned on the tree and surveyed the scene with an eagle eye. Much had taken place here and yet most of it had nothing to do with them, he thought.

Who were these two dead men? Why were their horses dead?

'It seems we've paid a damn high price for a

handful of maps, Captain,' Dubony said sadly.

Turner looked over his shoulder at the face of the trooper and knew his words echoed his own feelings exactly.

'Damn right, Clem. Damn right.'

The drums beat their continuous rhythm from high above the small party as slowly the men ventured out from their places of cover. There was a sickening warning in every vibrating beat as the percussion bounced off the rocks around the stream. Turner knew he had to keep alert because whatever they had ridden into, was far from over.

'Go and help Sam fill the water barrel, Clem,' Turner ordered as he wondered how much more of this carnage they could stomach.

EIGHTEEN

Could this be an Indian stronghold? Ward Jackson rubbed his sore eyes in disbelief at the sight which faced him. Edging his way down from the perilous corner of the rock-face, he suddenly found his feet on solid ground. Not just barren lifeless ground as he had expected but cultivated soil with crops stretching away into the distance to his right. This was land which was expertly irrigated from the cold pure mountain water; it was full of tall healthy crops in various stages of harvest.

Jackson walked slowly as if wondering when he would awake from this dream. Who were these people who had created this paradise up high amid the rocks of the towering mesa? Certainly these people did not fit into any category of Indian that Jackson had ever heard of.

No savage mind could have constructed this sophisticated water-distribution network, Ward Jackson thought. With every cautious step he could not help but marvel at the wondrous scene of ripe crops growing in almost military order beside him. It made no sense but he found himself drawn down the slight incline towards a narrow canyon full of majestic peaks and dozens of natural and man-made cave openings.

Could this be the place he had been looking for?

Ward Jackson sensed neither fear nor danger as he walked ever closer to what he took to be the heart of this strangely ordered society. Pausing to drink the cold water from a well-constructed irrigation sluice which trapped the never ceasing liquid as it ran down the rocks from somewhere high above, Jackson felt as if he had finally found what he had been seeking for so many long, hard years. Then he noticed something.

The drumming had stopped. Straightening up Jackson rubbed the refreshing water over his dry sun-baked features before seeing figures beginning to appear one by one.

Whoever these people were, they were quiet. Jackson felt the droplets of water dripping from his face as he stared at the growing gathering. Each and every one of these men, women and children were watching him, yet he still felt no fear.

He had seen Billy Charles killed instantly by one of these people's arrows and had been forced to run faster than he had ever thought possible to avoid meeting the same fate, yet he was unafraid.

Blinking as the water traced off his eyelashes and dripped on to his ragged clothes, Jackson found himself walking again straight towards the people who now were filling the narrow canyon ahead of him.

They were Indians all right, he thought. But different from any he had ever encountered in his twelve years of travelling on his relentless quest. Their faces held nothing but curiosity for the strange intruder who was approaching them.

Chief Shatashwa pushed his way through his people until he stood before them, watching the quiet man walking ever closer.

The old Indian's eyes narrowed as he tried to understand who the figure was. He had seen Apache warriors before many times over in his lifetime but this oddly attired creature was no Apache.

Shatashwa had seen Comanche and the occasional Cheyenne but this man was not one of them either. As Jackson drew even closer, the Pueblo chief could see the sparkling blue eyes beneath the rim of his hat.

For a brief instant the elderly Indian felt his heart miss a beat as he wondered if this could be a man at all. There were legends which told of beings from the happy hunting-ground who had magical powers bestowed upon them by the Great Spirit. Could this be such a being?

Shatashwa raised his hand and Jackson stopped a mere ten feet from him.

'Are you from the other world?'

Jackson listened to the strange language but could not understand a single word. He removed his hat and glanced into the fearful faces of the women and children before concentrating on the old men and finally Shatashwa himself.

'I can't say I understand you, mister, but I ain't hankering for no trouble,' Jackson said quietly.

The chief looked behind him at the faces of his people. He could not understand the words which were being spoken by the stranger but knew the voice held no danger in its tone.

Just then, high above them, Jackson caught sight of the deadly bowman who had killed Billy Charles moving over the rocks like a mountain goat. Before he could speak again, the sound of horses thundering up the narrow canyon behind them echoed about the mesa.

Shatashwa raised his right arm again and

turned. His people parted as the six horsemen drew their mounts to a stop outside the main cave.

Jackson stood as if rooted to the ground as he listened to the raised voices of the Pueblo. Whoever these battle-bruised braves were, they were not greeted like returning heroes. There was an anger in the chief's voice as he walked towards the dismounting men.

Talkana the medicine-man slid off the back of his pony and stood squarely before the approaching chief. His face seemed twisted by battle and defiant to all the furious words which met his return.

'I did warn you, Talkana. You promised these braves they would not come to any harm because you had endowed them with magic. I see many horses but where are my warriors?'

'You old woman.' Talkana spat at the feet of the chief. 'I went into battle whilst you stayed home and made blankets with the women. You dare question me?'

Shatashwa removed the long robe which covered his shoulders and tossed it to the ground between them.

'I told you if any of my young braves were harmed I would kill you with my bare hands. It seems I must kill you six times because your magic allowed at least six of our tribe to die.'

Talkana drew his knife from his belt and stood snarling at the older man.

'I fear you not, Shatashwa. This time my magic will overcome all your words. I shall kill you and I shall be the new chief of the Pueblo nation.'

The old chief began nodding as his hand found his tomahawk and drew it out from his belt. It had been many moons since he had held his trusty hatchet in anger but knew there was no other way of ending this evil creature's lust for power. Talkana had to be destroyed because he was a cancer who craved power, not for the good of his people but for self-satisfaction.

'There was a time when the Pueblo was indeed a nation, Talkana, but no longer. Now we are like the buffalo. We are few,' Chief Shatashwa stated as he felt the balance of his weapon in his hand.

'There shall be one less when I cut your heart from your breast, old man.' The medicine-man began to move sideways around the chief, clutching his knife in his bony grip.

Shatashwa remained in the same spot, shuffling his feet as he kept both eyes on the venomous-tongued Talkana.

'Are you afraid, Shatashwa?'

'There is an old saying, "it is a good day to fight, it is a good day to die". I have no fear of death,' the chief said as he held on to his trusty tomahawk and watched the thin-faced man before him. There was a silence on the mesa which seemed to chill the thin air around them.

'It is not I who shall die this day, it is you,' the medicine-man snarled as his eyes flashed up across the rocks above their heads.

'If the Great Spirit wills it, then it shall be.' Shatashwa nodded as he watched his opponent's every movement with eyes which had seen all kinds of horrors during his long life but none which turned his stomach the way Talkana did. 'I await your first move and hope it will be your last.'

Talkana glanced up at the highest point of the mesa where his brother Chokata knelt holding his lethal bow with the last of his deadly arrows poised for readiness. Signalling by waving his knife in the air, Talkana smiled as he saw his brother pulling back on the taut bow-string.

NINETEEN

Ward Jackson drew his pistol, and fanned its hammer twice as the archer released his lethal bow-string, sending the arrow down at Chief Shatashwa. The deafening noise of the gunshots rang out around the startled people of the mesa as his bullets found their mark. Chokata seemed to absorb both the bullets like a sponge before dropping his bow and falling from his high vantage point.

Every eye watched as Chokata's lifeless body dropped silently through the air before crashing onto the ground beside the stunned medicine-man. Talkana gazed down at his brother's body in total horror before twisting his thin neck around to seek out his executioner.

The vicious stare did not concern Ward

Jackson who had seen the signal from the knife-carrying man to the would-he assassin. Sliding his gun back into its holster silently, he walked though the shaking figures towards the wide-eyed Talkana, who seemed unable to believe his eyes.

Jackson passed the medicine-man and moved close to the chief who was staring at his bleeding arm and the arrow which had narrowly missed its target, stuck firmly into the ground at his feet.

Shatashwa stared into the blue eyes of the stranger and nodded his thanks to the man.

'Reckon that arrow kinda messed up your arm, Chief,' Jackson said, pointing to the bleeding gash which had made the chief drop his toma-hawk into the sand.

Shatashwa appeared to understand the mean-ing of Jackson's words as he watched him pluck-ing the tomahawk up from the ground before turning to face Talkana.

Jackson bit his lower lip as he studied the half-naked man clutching his knife.

'Reckon it's between you and me now, fella.'

The people of the Pueblo watched as Ward Jackson removed his gunbelt and handed it to the chief before pushing the injured man toward the crowd.

'This stranger is going to fight for Shatashwa,'

the voices began to say around the two men who faced one another over the chief's robe.

Talkana stared into the blue eyes and felt his blood run cold as he too remembered the legends of the magical beings who were sent by the Great Spirit in time of need to help the Pueblo people.

'Who is this creature, Shatashwa?' Talkana's voice questioned as he watched the calm figure facing him,

'He is someone who saved my life from the arrow of your brother, Talkana. An arrow which I suspect you ordered to find my heart,' the old chief replied as his wives began wrapping his wounded arm.

'This is no mere man. This is a messenger from the spirit world, Talkana,' Fetina the elder shouted at the medicine-man as he waved the women to assist his wounded chief. 'Look at his eyes, Talkana. Are they not like the sky? Do you not recognize one whom you have prayed to?'

Talkana's eyes darted around the gathering. 'This must be one of the intruders.'

'But how could he have reached here before you? No, Talkana, this is no intruder, this is the one who it was long ago written would come to help our people.' Shatashwa smiled at the medicine-man.

'Are you gonna fight or just confab?' Jackson

asked Talkana as he crouched down clutching at the strange hatchet in his hands.

Talkana stared around the faces of the Pueblo and could see the hatred carved into them. Then he looked at the strange intruder opposite him. A man who was waiting to fight another man's battle for him.

Would a stranger be willing to risk death for someone he had only just met? Perhaps a man would not, but a messenger from the spirit world might.

The medicine-man sucked in air and lowered his head as he summoned all his strength to assist him. Moving forward be began to swing the deadly blade before him, waiting to see fear in the face of Jackson.

Jackson began to smile.

Talkana raised his knife and lunged at his opponent. Jackson moved with all the skill of a matador and watched as the Indian fell to the ground.

'You shall die, blue eyes,' Talkana snarled as he quickly got to his feet and grabbed Jackson around the middle. Both men clutched the other's arms as they gritted their teeth and tumbled across the flat ground through the watching crowd. Jackson managed to free one of his hands and threw a well-aimed fist into the belly of the medicine-man.

144

As Talkana staggered backward he slashed his razor-sharp blade across Jackson's left arm. Blood began to run down from the wound and trace across his knuckles.

'I wish you hadn't gone and done that, friend,' Ward Jackson spat as he kicked the Indian's legs from under him.

Talkana rolled down a slight incline and found himself beneath the hoofs of one of the Apache ponies. As he desperately tried to clamber out as he saw Ward Jackson racing toward him, the horse began to buck.

Jackson gave the tomahawk in his hand a glance and then discarded it before leaping on to the rising man. Now he had both hands free, Jackson felt as if he could use his superior weight to wrestle the smaller man into submission.

The two grappling men crashed into the group of startled ponies and somehow managed to roll between the legs without being kicked by the unshod hooves.

As Jackson held the right hand of Talkana firmly he felt the blade of the knife again find his flesh. This time the pain was in his shoulder as the deadly point ripped through his jacket and tore at his skin.

Once more Jackson clenched his fist and hit the face of the medicine-man. Once again there appeared to be no effect on the stone-faced Talkana as they continued rolling across the ground towards the edge of the high mesa. The crowd which followed them remained silent as they kept up with the deadly duel.

Jackson hit the jaw of the Indian with every ounce of his strength and felt Talkana gasp and weaken. Swiftly, Jackson got back on to his feet and watched the face below him start to rise once again. He had never seen such a face before. There was an evil in its features which frightened the trail-weary man. Yet, Ward Jackson had always faced his fears square on.

Stepping backward as he balanced himself again, Jackson felt some rocks touching the spurs on his high-heeled boots. Glancing down he suddenly saw the fifty-foot sheer drop. Jackson gulped and stepped away from the cliff edge just as Talkana got back to his feet once more.

'You ain't gonna quit, are you?' Jackson said as he watched the medicine-man rush at him with his knife-blade leading the way. Jackson moved sideways and brought his left leg up until his knee caught his adversary in the chest.

Talkana gasped and fell to his knees beside the bleeding Jackson. Even winded, the Indian still had enough energy left to lash out with the blood-stained blade.

Ward Jackson felt the honed blade slicing through the side of his left boot as he tried to move away. The cut was clean and true but had not touched his flesh this time. Jackson gasped as he carefully walked away from the determined medicine-man, who once again rose up to his full height.

Jackson looked around the faces of the Indians who were watching at a respectful distance before he turned his attention back on to the knife-wielding warrior.

'You are no spirit, blue eyes,' Talkana said as he closed in on his antagonist again. 'Only men bleed. You are a mere man and I shall destroy you.'

Jackson could not understand the ranting which spewed from Talkana's mouth but he had a pretty good idea what the man was saying. Looking at his left hand, Jackson saw the blood dripping freely from under his sleeve and shook his arm. It was beginning to stiffen up as the wide-eyed screaming Talkana charged into him heavily.

The knife-blade flashed before Jackson's face as they tumbled over the uneven ground closer and closer to the perilous cliff edge. Clutching at the hand which held the knife, Jackson felt his bleeding arm weaken and give.

The blade swept across him, ripping into his

jacket front and snagging on the coarse material.

Jackson closed his eyes and butted the medicine-man on his nose as he desperately clawed his way from the Indian. The sound of the nose breaking seemed to ring around the assembled audience as blood squirted from Talkana's face. Holding on to his knife-handle firmly, Talkana felt the blade shredding Jackson's jacket-front.

The blue-eyed man somehow managed to get back on to his feet and stagger towards the discarded tomahawk. He had tried to be noble but knew this Indian was one man who could not be bested by mere blows on the chin, however accurately they were dispatched.

Ward Jackson wearily snatched the hatchet up from the ground and stood watching as the grim-faced Talkana started towards him yet again. At least now he had the pleasure of seeing his opponent's face covered in blood.

'I will pluck your blue eyes from your head and then slowly I shall kill you,' Talkana blazed as his feet found momentum and his dagger began to glisten in the rays of the sun.

Raising the tomahawk quickly, Jackson caught the elbow of the crazed brave as he side-stepped the flashing blade. Blood splattered across the air from the gash underneath Talkana's arm as he stopped and jabbed his knife furiously.

Jackson smashed his tomahawk across the bloodstained blade as it sought out his heart. Talkana paused for a moment and looked at his own blood, now dripping on to the sand. He narrowed his eyes as he began to scream at the heavens.

The bleeding Ward Jackson moved fearfully away from the maniacal Talkana as exhaustion and blood-loss began to take their toll on him. Simply holding the tomahawk across his middle as he felt his blood draining from his body took every ounce of Jackson's remaining strength. Now it was only will power which kept him upright as he faced the haunting man before him.

Talkana began to approach slowly this time.

There was a totally different look etched upon his terrifying features.

Jackson blinked hard. He felt his vision beginning to fail him as he held on to the tomahawk. He had been in many a tight spot over the years but nothing which came close to this one.

The sun bounced off the skin of the medicine-man as he moved closer and closer with slow forceful steps. Jackson felt himself instinctively backing away.

Then it appeared that no matter how hard he blinked, he could not focus on the man or the deadly knife which bore down on him.

Like a mountain lion leaping at its prey, Talkana seemed to fly across the distance between them. Jackson could not see anything clearly as the figure sprang at him. All he could see was a menacing blur.

As he attempted to raise the hatchet, Jackson felt his knees give way and he slumped on to the ground as the figure passed over him. Talkana's knee caught him in the face and sent him sprawling on to his spine.

It was only then that he heard the pitiful cry of the man who was falling to his death down the side of the high mesa wall.

Rolling slowly on to his stomach, Ward Jackson looked over the edge of the cliff down into the distant abyss. It was over, he thought, as he suddenly became aware of numerous hands helping him up off the ground. Hands which would tend his wounds and ask for nothing in return.

FINALE

Captain Joel Turner watched the surrounding brush as well as the high mesa tensely as burly corporal Sam Hyde secured the wooden lid back on to the water barrel. The drumming had stopped at least an hour earlier but he felt no relief in the silence which had replaced the chilling noise. All the cavalry officer could think of was getting out of here as quickly as possible but there were limits to how fast this could be achieved.

Trooper Clem Dubony nervously assisted Hyde in hitching the four-horse team back into their traces. As they worked with the refreshed horses, both men kept a vigilant eye out for danger, which they knew could strike from anywhere in this place. The two dead mounts which lay close to the bodies of Duke Walker and Billy Charles were now attracting flies. In normal circumstances Turner would have ordered the dead men to be properly buried and the carcasses of the dead mounts dragged out into the desert for the carrion to feed off. Yet this was no normal situation that he presided over; this was probably the most dangerous place he had ever found himself cornered in.

Somehow the map maker Byron Gregory appeared to have forgotten everything which had occurred. He sat on the wagon tail-gate continually sketching the compelling scenery for future reference and addition to his thick files of maps.

Turner moved alongside the talented artist and stared at the impressive drawing before speaking.

'You are the coolest customer I've ever come across, Mr Gregory. Doesn't anything ever worry you?'

'I happen to be scared beyond your wildest imaginings, Captain Turner,' Gregory answered as he continued adding subtle touches to his work.

'You hide it well,' Turner said as be pulled down the brim of his hat and stared up at the adobes.

Gregory paused and looked straight into the eyes of the man next to him. 'I've witnessed more horror in the past month than I saw in the whole of my life prior to setting out on this fateful expedition. I have taken another man's life and am truly sickened by this place. For all I know a band of hostile aborigines are going to attack us at any moment and the thought terrifies me, Captain. So I continue to do the only thing I am good at and that is drawing and making maps. But I am scared, dear sir. Do not think otherwise.'

Turner sighed and patted the man on his arm. 'You better prepare for us heading out of here real fast, Mr Gregory. The boys have almost got the wagon team readied and when they are ready, hang on for dear life.'

The map maker folded the pages of his sketch-pad until they were protected by the hand-tooled pigskin cover. Then he jumped down, turned and pushed up the wooden tail-gate. He secured the metal pins on either side.

'The team is hitched up, Captain,' Sam Hyde said as the long-legged officer approached him, still watching for danger from all around them.

'Have all our horses been fed?' Turner asked.

'Clem and me fed all of them, sir,' the big man responded as he watched the young trooper wading out into the stream to gather up the reins to his and the officers' horses.

'Then let's try and make a real quiet exit from

153

this damn place before them Indians decide to use us for target practice.' The captain nodded as he began heading towards Dubony who was leading their mounts back to dry land.

Just as Byron Gregory had reached the high driver's seat on the wagon the sound of drumming started again. As Hyde climbed up beside him and gathered the heavy leather reins in his huge hands he spat.

'I knew them varmints weren't licked.'

Captain Joel Turner dragged his mount from the stream slightly ahead of Dubony. Both exhausted soldiers looked at each other sceptically as the sound of the drumming filled their heads again.

'Not again.' Dubony began to shake as he mounted his horse.

There was no emotion in the face of the captain as he led his horse silently back towards the wagon.

'Captain?' Hyde's voice broke through the veneer which masked the officer's silence.

'Take it easy, boys,' Turner said as he pushed his foot into his stirrup and hauled himself on to the back of his horse. 'We ain't gonna lose this one. Let them come if they dare.'

The trooper rode up beside the straight-backed Turner and pleaded with the man. 'I've had it, sir. I wanna ride out of this damn place.'

'Easy, Clem. You're not the only man around here whose guts are twisted into a knot,' Turner told the trooper as he pulled his mount full circle and faced the wagon. 'Turn this team around, Sam. We better head out darn fast.'

The crusty corporal nodded and dragged the heavy reins hard to his left as his foot kicked off the brake pole. Slowly the battle-scarred vehicle began to turn as the four horses pulled it around the small space close to the stream. It was a difficult manoeuvre even for the skilled hands of Sam Hyde.

Turner sat in his saddle listening to the drums as he waited patiently for the creaking prairie schooner to come full about behind him. With each beat of the drums, Dubony seemed to cringe as if he expected an arrow to find his trembling torso. Only the strength of the officer kept the younger man from spurring his horse away.

Finally the wagon managed to complete the awkward turn and Hyde began to straighten his team up behind the two waiting outriders.

As Captain Turner began to raise his white gauntlet, a cloud of dust passed before their horses. It seemed an eternity as the tired eyes of the soldiers waited until the small group of riders came into view.

Chief Shatashwa rode beside the wounded

Ward Jackson ahead of three Pueblo elders into the clearing. Face to face with what remained of the army troop, the riders stopped their ponies.

Dubony reached for his pistol but found Turner's gloved hand poised above his holster.

'They got a white man with them, Captain!'

Turner said nothing as he urged his horse forward towards the riders.

Ward Jackson slid carefully from the back of the Indian pony and walked toward the startled officer, who immediately dismounted.

'You're not a hostage?' Turner asked Jackson.

'Nope.' Jackson forced a smile as he stopped. 'As far as I've been able to figure, these Indians are a peaceful tribe, Captain.'

Turner pointed down at the body of Fred White beneath the large tree. 'Peaceful? Look at my dead trooper.'

Jackson continued. 'The critter who stirred up the young braves is dead. Him and me had us a fight, and as you can see, I nearly lost.'

The eyes of the officer focused on Jackson's wounds.

'I don't understand, stranger.'

'The name's Ward Jackson, Captain. It's a long story but I found myself up on that mesa just in time to save the life of the chief here. These people ain't looking to hurt you.'

156

Turner stared up into the face of the chief, who sat proudly atop his pony.

'You mean we can go without any further trouble?'

Jackson nodded and pointed to a heavily laden pony beside the chief. 'I got them to bring some fresh crops down from their fields for you.'

'Crops?' The officer seemed confused. 'I never heard of any Indians who farmed crops before.'

'Until an hour or so back, neither had I.' Ward Jackson forced a smile which belied his wounds. 'But these ain't like no other Indians I've ever heard of. All they seek is to be left alone and free of trouble.'

Captain Turner shook his head as he thought of their mission.

'We are a map-making expedition, Mr Jackson. I'm afraid, once we return north, this place and these people will no longer be unknown.'

Jackson's face went suddenly grim as he thought about those who would follow once maps of this land became public property.

'There ain't many of these folks left now, Captain. If others come here it might mark the end of them altogether.'

Turner shook his head. 'There is nothing I can do. . . .'

Byron Gregory tossed his book of detailed

sketches at the feet of the two men.

'That is the only record of this place, gentlemen, do with it what you will.'

Captain Joel Turner picked up the book and then handed it to Chief Shatashwa. The Indian warrior held the book in his hands and opened it and studied the pictures.

'Are you sure, Mr Gregory?'

'As far as I'm concerned this place does not exist,' came the reply.

'Then there will be no maps, Mr Jackson,' Turner sighed.

Ward Jackson walked to the pony with the fresh crops upon its back and removed the large bundle. He walked to the wagon and handed it up to Gregory.

'Thanks, Mr Gregory.'

The map maker accepted the crops and smiled down at the blue-eyed injured man who made his way back to his bareback pony and managed to mount it.

'You are staying with these people, Mr Jackson?' Turner asked as he stepped into his stirrup and hauled himself back onto his saddle.

Ward Jackson held on to the mane of the pony and grinned at the four faces in turn.

'I've spent a dozen years looking for someplace

where I might actually be useful. Reckon this is it, Captain.'

'Are you sure?'

'Is any man sure of his destiny, Captain?' Jackson turned the pony and rode surrounded by the silent Pueblo braves back into the dense brush which fringed the base of the great natural monolith.

As the covered wagon and its two dishevelled outriders began crossing the desert the fiery sun started to set. Turner stared over his shoulder and looked at the crimson sky behind the gigantic rock, and began to wonder about the man called Ward Jackson.

But mostly he could not help but marvel at the mysterious mesa which stood defiantly, as it had done since time began.